The Boy Who Lived In A Tree

By

Mitch Martin

authorHOUSE

1663 Liberty Drive, Suite 200
Bloomington, Indiana 47403
(800) 839-8640
www.authorhouse.com

© 2004 Mitch Martin.
All Rights Reserved.

First published by AuthorHouse 07/01/04

ISBN: 1-4184-3427-2 (sc)

Library of Congress Control Number: 2004094017

This book is printed on acid-free paper.

Printed in the United States of America
Bloomington, Indiana

To my wife Candi, it would not have been possible without your help and encouragement. To my children, Jennifer and Jon, always remember the importance of family and heritage.

With fondest memories of the countless hours I spent listening intently to my parents, Darrell and Amy Martin, as well as aunts and uncles and neighbors recounting the stories passed down from generation to generation. Particularly, my Uncle Charley and Aunt Lula Belle Crow.

And to every child who has ever daydreamed of surviving alone in the forest.

Chapter One

It was late afternoon, but there was no way to tell. The sky was gray from horizon to horizon. The trees had lost most of their leaves or there would have been no horizon to see. It was mid-November, damp, chilly, and occasionally the constant drizzle would swell into a light, cold rain.

The boy would walk and sometimes trot, but after six days of the same weather and the same gait, there was more walking than trotting. He had crossed the White River--just below the trading post run by some folks named Schell[1], near where the James River joined with the White River-- late on the second day. He had purposefully avoided the post, wanting no one to see him. There were few white people located between the White River and the Buffalo Fork[2], and not many Indians either.

A lot of ground can be covered in six days of constant travel, stopping only to sleep from dark to dawn. He had been lucky to find a few hickory nuts and the occasional walnut along the way, the precious few nuts that the squirrels had missed. Occasionally a persimmon tree[3] would yield a few sweet fruits that had not yet fallen or been picked by hungry forest creatures. Yesterday he had found a chinquapin[4] tree, the ground

1

covered with the spiny burr-covered husks that protected the sweet nuts. He had stopped long enough to peel a couple of handfuls of nuts out of the husks and stuff them into the small canvas sack that hung around his neck and over one shoulder. The sack contained his meager possessions: a pair of britches and a shirt only slightly less threadbare than the ones he wore; a piece of flint and a bar of steel wrapped in buckskin; a small knife with a five-inch blade, also wrapped in buckskin; and a greasy rag that covered a small piece of smoked pork that was covered in lint and the crumbs of long-ago eaten cornbread.

He had eaten the last of the cornbread the night before, and some of the nuts, then washed it all down with lots of water from a small, clear stream. After that, he'd curled up in some dry leaves under a rock overhang cut eons ago by the same stream. The gangly dog that traveled with him had curled up beside him, pressing his bony body as close to the boy as possible. The warmth was welcome, but the smell of the wet dog was less inviting. The dog had obviously found a less palatable evening meal than the boy had, at least from a human perspective. "Every rose has its thorn, David," he remembered his mother saying as a tear made an attempt at cleaning a path down his cheek.

What a difference a week could make in your life, he thought. He had been young, only eight, when his mother and baby sister had died, soon after the birth of the latter. He and his father had been devastated, and had relied heavily on each other in order to survive. That had been the first time his life had changed completely in only a week. He could remember the excitement as the time grew near for the birth of his sibling. He had been allowed to join in the process of preparing for the arrival. His father had wanted the name Darrell if a son was born, after his own little brother, whom they didn't get to see often enough.

Darrell had found a place to settle that he had been very excited about, and a girl to share it with. When he had last visited about two years ago, he had tried very hard to convince David's dad to join him. The valley was only a few days' travel to the south. Great farmland just for the taking, no inhabitants except the occasional Indian hunting party, and lots of game. As soon as his cabin was completed, he was going back to Shawnee Town[5] on the White River to pick up his new bride and have her settled in before winter. He had explained carefully how to find his new place. Uncle Darrell was loved by both of David's parents, and a hero to David. He was always full of stories of great hunts, and trips to trade with faraway Indian villages. His tales of skirmishes with hostile Indians kept you on the edge of the chair, and his description of faraway lands created visions of milk and honey of almost Biblical proportions. He had tried his best to get David's father to come join him, but David's father had been reluctant to uproot David so soon after his mother's death. David also suspected that he was reluctant to travel so far away from her grave as well.

Now, after his father's untimely death, he needed desperately to find Uncle Darrell. There was no way that he could stay in the settlement and live with the family that the constable had appointed as his guardian and caretaker. They were much too eager to move their brood in and take control of David's home and all of his family's meager possessions. Helen, the constable's sister, had recently arrived with her lazy husband, brood of children, and not many other possessions, in a rickety wagon pulled by two sickly-looking horses. David's father's untimely death had created an opportunity for them to obtain all they needed before winter set in.

David had been immediately relegated to the barn loft as living quarters, and most of his clothes and bedding were given to the children of the new caretakers. He was gone before daylight the first morning, with no opportunity to get inside the house to reclaim even his coat.

This day was no different than the previous five of David's travel, except he was more tired, hungrier, and so far, had found nothing from nature's garden to supplement his meager fare. Every hickory tree he passed showed evidence of squirrels feasting on a plentiful crop, but what hadn't been eaten had been buried away for later use. The few nuts that he found always contained a small hole in one end and had one or more fat white grubs chewing away inside. He soon learned to not waste his time cracking them open. The squirrels must have been able to smell the worms and knew not to waste their time either.

He was starting to worry; he was almost out of food, and well past the point of no return. He had no gun to kill the plentiful squirrels, the numerous turkey or deer.[6] The deer and turkey were having a feast on acorns, but these were far too bitter for the human palate. He had heard that the Indians ate them, but he didn't understand how. Maybe they boiled them or cooked them some other way.

Aside from the small canvas sack that flopped at his side with every step, he carried a small single bit axe in his left hand. It was bigger than a hatchet or tomahawk, but smaller than one normally used by a woodcutter. It was the small axe that his mother had kept at the woodpile behind the house for splitting bigger pieces of wood into smaller sticks to be used for kindling or the cook fire. Since he didn't have a gun, the axe gave him a small amount of comfort as a weapon against a chance encounter with a bear or an unfriendly Indian. Slim comfort, but better than nothing.

He carried a sling in his pocket, like the one his namesake had used to slay the giant Goliath. That, along with a half dozen specially selected rocks, was always in his pocket. Having played with and practiced with the sling since he was four or five years old, he could use it very effectively against small game. More than once he had killed rabbits while they were sitting still around the edge of the cornfield thinking they were hidden in the shadows.

He had also killed passenger pigeons[7] when a huge flock had flown over their cabin to roost in the dense pines and cedars on the hill behind their home. Once he had hurled an egg-sized rock into the flock and brought down three birds with the first stone, reloaded with a second rock and brought down two more. His mother had cut off the heads and feet and removed the entrails. She had then covered the entire bird with mud that David had mixed up with loose soil from the vegetable garden and a bucket of water from the spring. The mud-covered birds were then placed in the back corner of the fireplace and covered with hot coals. A couple of hours later, the family ate the best supper he could remember.

He had been only seven, but he could remember his father saying to his mother that David was going to be a good provider, that he was already helping to feed the family, and with the family "fixing to grow," he would be glad for the help. David wondered what he meant about the family growing, but hadn't wanted to spoil the moment by asking. His mother had cracked the hard balls of clay on the edge of the hearth and peeled away the clay which had stuck to the feathers and skin of the birds, leaving the steaming, succulent flesh cleaned and ready to eat. They had boiled carrots and turnips from the root cellar with fresh butter melting over the top, a steaming pan of cornbread fresh from the Dutch oven, and a bowl of wild greens that his mother had picked and boiled through two changes of water.

What a meal that had been; he could remember every detail. Why, when he was so hungry, was food the only thing he could think about? He snapped back to the present after remembering the big mug of ice-cold milk dipped from the stone crock that sat immersed in water in the stone spring house. His mother had been very proud of her Guernsey milk cow.

It was now late in the afternoon, and David was starting to catch glimpses of sunlight streaming through the thinning clouds over the hills to the west. Good, he was still going south. Without the sun to guide him, he was not always sure about his direction of travel, but his instincts and sense of direction were good. He figured he must be close to 60 or 70 miles south of the settlement with no sign of pursuit. The game trails he followed showed no sign of human travel. He noticed that the sky was clearing and the wind was now coming from the northwest. The temperature was dropping noticeably; he shivered and tried to get back into a trot. Old Smokey, always the leader, had stopped far ahead to look back at him as if to ask which way to go.

The game trail had forked; one fork skirted the big hill to the south and the other fork followed the slope off to the west. The thing about game trails, they always follow the easiest path. West was straight over the top of the hill, but game trails never went straight up a hill. He chose the left track, hoping to keep the hill between himself and the cold northwest wind. Smokey loped on ahead after the direction of travel was determined. He always had to be the leader.

David realized that it was going to be a very cold night, the coldest since he had left home. He needed to find a cozy place where he could build a fire for the night. Wood was plentiful, but wet. He was out of tinder for starting a fire; it would be difficult to start one without some dry material like an old bird's nest. If he couldn't get a fire started, he might very well freeze to death. Suddenly he didn't seem so hungry. He quickened his pace as he noticed the sun was about to drop from sight over the high hill. It was already getting dark as the sun disappeared below the top of the hill, and the temperature dropped noticeably in the shadow formed by the hill.

He noticed that Smokey had his nose to the ground and was excitedly circling back and forth under some persimmon trees. David knew he was trying to work out the trail of some animal. He realized he could be in trouble if Smokey took off after game and was gone all night; his one source of warmth would not be there to keep him alive. David was startled as Smokey gave an excited yelp and took off in a dead run. He was on the trail of something and that something must not be very far ahead. The one time an animal will not seek the easiest route is when it is being pursued. This critter was obviously making a beeline for safer territory. Within seconds, Smokey was out of sight over the shoulder of the hill. David heard one more yelp in the distance. He headed in that direction. Smokey was a mixed-breed dog, commonly called a cur. Unlike a hound, whose instinct was to bay as he followed a trail with his nose, his instinct was to pursue and catch whatever he was after with little fanfare. His nose worked very well, but if he were close enough to see his intended quarry, he followed by sight and wasted no energy on barking.

David took off toward the last yelp as fast as he could go. It was dark enough that he had trouble seeing the saw briars and wait-a-minute vines that sought to hold him back. When he reached the lower ground along a stream after crossing over the hill, the vegetation became more and more dense. Thick underbrush and wild cane were making it almost impossible to penetrate. Sobbing with panic and gasping for breath, he came to a stop at the edge of a small river. He tried to control his breathing in order to hear any sounds of pursuit. It was difficult to hear over his pounding heart and labored breathing.

From upstream, there came the distant sounds of a vicious battle. There was barking, growling, hissing, and yelping, a terrifying din that sound like a battle to the death. Once again, David took off as fast as his fatigued body would allow. It sounded like Smokey needed some help; if it were a bobcat or a mountain lion, he wasn't sure there was much he could do. Smokey might be a match for a smaller bobcat, but not a much larger mountain lion. He hoped Smokey hadn't bit off more than he could chew. A steep bluff was on David's right and the steep stream bank was on his left. The space between the two was getting narrower as he went further upstream. There were large boulders that almost blocked his path. Some were taller than he was and nearly filled the area between the bluff and stream. Total darkness had descended; there was no moon. A few stars occasionally peeked their way through the clouds.

He stopped once again to listen for sounds that would direct him to the battle. It was very quiet. Suddenly, only a few yards in front of him was a thrashing sound, followed by a strangled cry that was almost human. Eerie silence followed. David crept forward with his axe raised, watching for movement. In front of him, and completely blocking his progress was a giant tree that filled the entire gap between bluff and stream bank. The tree was wider than his outstretched arms, and towering above him were the ghostly white branches that gleamed against the faint skylight cast by the few stars.

The river bank was at least ten feet high and a white mass of roots from the old sycamore were exposed, hanging down like giant tentacles from a landlocked octopus. A large boulder had fallen many years ago, and was wedged between the tree and the bluff. The tree had grown partially around the boulder, sealing it tightly between itself and the bluff. He crept forward, looking for a way around the tree. There seemed no way, except to attempt to climb over the huge rock. That would be difficult in daylight, impossible at night. Looking closely at the base of the rock, he saw there seemed to be a small cave or depression under the rock. Getting down on his hands and knees, he realized he was in a narrow game trail that disappeared under the rock.

He crawled forward and discovered a passage under the rock big enough for him to crawl through. There were a few faint noises coming from the far side of the tree. David had no choice but to squeeze through the opening, careful to keep his axe in front. He finally made it to the far side of the tree. He was scraped and bruised, bleeding from several superficial cuts. He could make out the figure of Smokey, very faintly outlined against the tree. He was standing stiff-legged with a slightly squirming mass of fur grasped firmly in his jaws. A final sharp side-to-side shake seemed to finally stop the movements of the large critter that he had captured.

After catching his breath, David laid down his axe and patted Smokey on the back. The dog relaxed and released his grip on the throat of his quarry, then stood panting with his tongue hanging out, looking very pleased with his accomplishment. The critter was obviously dead. David prodded it with his foot and realized from the ringed tail that it was a huge raccoon. It was the largest 'coon that he had ever seen. It looked like both he and Smokey would eat very well tonight. That is, if he could get a fire started.

David took off his canvas pack and laid it down on a flat rock with his axe, then started searching for material with which to build a fire. After four days of almost continuous rain, this could be a chore. He searched along the edge of the bluff's entire length until the bluff and river merged another 50 yards upstream. The river made a bend away from the bluff just past the huge sycamore, then curved back about 50 yards further upstream, leaving an almost inaccessible piece of land between. The bluff was sheer at the base and offered no overhang to shelter any leaves or dry twigs. There were plenty of tree limbs and fallen dead timber for fuel, but he could find nothing dry in the dark. He really wished that he had spent time earlier in the day looking for some tinder to carry with him.

As the sweat from his exertion began to dry, he was becoming more and more chilled. He made his way back to the tree, and in a panic, with his teeth chattering, started looking around the base of the tree for a bit of sheltered dry material. He realized suddenly there was a good-sized hole in the side of the tree. Obviously the 'coon had been making for the safety of his lair when Smokey had caught him at the very entrance. He began feeling around inside the opening in the tree, where he found dry leaves and twigs. The hole was big enough to crawl into, but there was no telling what other creatures might be using it for a den.

He grabbed up a handful of the dry litter and began rolling and crumbling it into fine fibers that might catch a spark and ignite. He accumulated a small nest-shaped pile in the sheltered opening of the tree, got out his flint and steel, and started striking sparks. His hands were so cold that they were stiff and clumsy. After numerous attempts, he was rewarded with a big spark that landed in the right place and continued to glow. David leaned down and blew gently on the spark. At last, there was a tiny tendril of smoke and then a tiny flame. He carefully moved a couple of strands of material close to the flame and continued to blow gently as the flame grew. Hope of warmth and a full belly grew with it.

Chapter Two

The raccoon was carefully skinned and cleaned. Smokey waited patiently for his share and seemed perfectly content with the offal and the head, which David split with his axe to give him easy access to the nourishment inside.

David carefully moved the small fire to a bare, rocky spot of ground a couple of feet from the bluff. He went back to the tree and gathered more dry material, sticks and leaves, to feed the fire. He knew that he could burn even damp wood after he had a good hot fire going. By crawling partway into the hole, David was able to retrieve plenty of dry material. He then began to drag bigger limbs and logs back to the fire. Some he placed on top of the fire, others he stacked up close enough to start the drying process as the fire got bigger.

He cut the 'coon up into six pieces, separating the legs from the torso and the remaining back into two pieces. He placed the meat on some clean, flat rocks positioned near the fire, then sat down to rest and wait for it to cook. He was still chilled and was tempted to build up the fire by adding more wood. However, common sense prevailed; this was Indian country, and a big fire could be seen from a long distance. A smaller fire would also mean gathering less wood.

The fire was starting to feel very good as the warmth reflected off the surface of the bluff behind it. He was very tired and hungry, and his clothes were finally starting to dry. He felt that he probably had plenty of wood stacked by the fire to last all night; if he conserved his fuel, he should not have to find more before daybreak. He was starting to relax for the first time since leaving home, and he had time to think. He decided that he had traveled far enough to be safe from pursuit, so he might rest for a few days and try to build up some supplies. With cold weather arriving, he desperately needed some furs to augment his meager wardrobe. He didn't even have a coat. The raccoon was a start; maybe there were more 'coons inside the den in the hollow tree.

Impulsively, he grabbed a burning tree branch. Using it for a torch, he pushed it through the opening into the huge tree. Holding it in one hand, he crawled into the opening. To his surprise, the opening was very large. He moved all of his body into the cavity, and slowly raised his makeshift torch high above his head. A ceiling did not seem to exist; the huge cavity extended out of sight above the light cast by his flickering flame. Slowly, he stood to his full height; he could neither touch nor see anything above his head. A quick look around showed the opening to be wider than his height. It was dry and littered with the remnants of nesting materials of various animals. It showed many years of use as a den. Old bones littered the floor; most were ancient and well-gnawed, but a few looked to be of more recent vintage.

Smokey suddenly crawled through the opening and started sniffing around. There was obviously a storybook of tantalizing smells, but no indication from him that there were currently any inhabitants. The flame at the end of David's tree branch was almost extinguished, so he crawled back through the opening to check on his supper. Smokey seemed content to stay inside for the present.[8]

The meat was starting to sizzle in its own juices, and the tantalizing smell overwhelmed David with hunger. He added more fuel to the fire and turned the meat with his fingers, slightly burning himself in the process. After a few more minutes, he could no longer resist, and took one of the smaller front quarters of meat and bounced it back and forth between his hands until it was cool enough to hold. He burned his mouth with the first bite of the tough old 'coon, but he gladly suffered through the pain to chew his first bite of fresh hot food in several days. Had it not been for good old Smokey, he might not have made it this far. He looked around for the faithful dog, but Smokey was still inside the hollow tree. Smokey's belly was full with his share of the 'coon, so he was probably taking a nap and licking his wounds from the battle.

David started eating his second piece of meat, then realized that he had better save the rest. More meat could be difficult to obtain and he needed to stretch what he had for as many days as possible. The second piece was cooked more thoroughly but was just as tough and gamey as the first. In spite of this, it was one of the best meals David could remember. Hunger can make the palate less discriminating. As he finished the second piece of meat, he removed the remaining pieces from the fire. When they had cooled--which happened rapidly in the freezing wind that was now whistling through the trees--David wrapped them in his greasy rag with the bit of salt pork and stored them in his canvas bag.

He was suddenly very tired, but the cold wind was so penetrating that he couldn't stay comfortable without hovering over the fire. Once again, he looked around for Smokey, who still hadn't come out of the tree. Even with the fire, he would need the dog's warmth to make it through the night. If he went to sleep and the fire went out, he might not wake up. He took his spare set of clothes from his bag and put them on over the clothes he wore. That helped a little, but not very much. His hands froze if he took them from his pockets, and his face and ears were getting raw from the wind.

He went to the opening of the hollow tree and called to Smokey, but got no response. He started to panic; maybe the dog had come out while he was eating and he had not seen him. He grabbed another burning limb and once again crawled inside the tree. Lying on a thick pile of leaves on the far side of the opening, Smokey raised a sleepy head to look up at David for a second, then snuggled back into his pile of leaves. The dog was comfortably curled up on the leaves with his tail curled around his body and his nose tucked under the tip of his tail. He seemed uninterested in being any other place.

David noticed that out of the wind, it seemed much warmer inside the tree. He could even feel the heat from the flame of the small torch. Seeing the wisdom of the dog's actions, David scraped an area clean of leaf litter. Using his torch, he ignited a small fire of dry twigs and bark. He soon had a cheery little fire going on the bare ground inside the tree. Smoke from the fire rose straight up, indicating that there was a place for it to escape from the tree cavity somewhere above. The glow of the fire gave him a better view of his surroundings, and he realized that this was where he should spend the night. A tiny fire would keep the small area very cozy, and he would be out of the wind and out of sight. He added a little more fuel to his small fire and crawled back out. In a few minutes, he had extinguished the fire outside and moved all of his belongings and his stack of wood inside. He piled several sticks of wood over the opening to discourage any unwelcome intruders, and was soon asleep next to Smokey.

Chapter Three

Throughout the long night, David awoke when the fire died down, added a few sticks of wood, and promptly went back to sleep. Smokey licking his face abruptly brought him to reality. The fire had burned down to just a few glowing coals, and he could barely make out the shape of the dog standing over him. He reached over and threw a handful of leaves on the coals, which smoked for a few seconds then burst into flame. Adding a few small sticks, he had the fire blazing merrily in minutes.

Smokey had meanwhile gone to the opening and waited patiently for David to remove the wood he had placed over it. David realized the dog needed to go outside, and his own full bladder reminded him that he needed to as well. It seemed to still be very dark outside; there was no sign of light coming through the opening. David removed the wood and discovered that it had snowed during the night. There was a pile of snow behind the wood, completely filling the opening into the tree. David used a long piece of wood to poke through the opening to the outside. A little light entered.

Smokey pushed on through the opening, plowing through the snow to the outside. David followed into a world transformed white. There was at least a foot of snow covering everything. The wind had caused drifts to form around obstacles, hiding the shape of any object that it encountered. Smokey wasted no time relieving himself; he then drank from a clear pool of water that had collected in a depression at the base of the bluff. A small trickle of water ran down the face of the bluff; icicles were forming on the bluff and dripping ice cold water into the small pool.

David answered the call of nature, drank a few handfuls of icy water, and followed Smokey back into the tree. It was still snowing hard enough to soften the outline of his tracks in the very short time he was outside. He replaced the wood over the opening and, gauging the size of his woodpile, placed one small stick on the fire. Smokey curled back up in the warm leaves and left David to worry about this dangerous turn of events.

David was in no way prepared for this early blizzard. It often snowed before Christmas, but not this much so early in the season. In his 12 years of experience, he only remembered autumn snows of a few inches that were gone in a few days. A warm-up, along with cold but sunny fall days, usually followed these small snowstorms. He thought about stories he had listened to, told by the older folks, that talked of winters they had experienced when the snow came early and stayed on the ground until spring. A winter like that could be the end of him. David sat by the fire and worried, slowly feeding his small supply of wood into the tiny fire. Before the day was over, he would have to go out into the snow and gather more wood. He was not looking forward to that cold experience. He couldn't envision how to find game in this blizzard. Any chance of finding more nuts had also vanished under the blanket of snow.

A body can only sit by the fire and worry for so long, so David decided it was time for some action. After all, idle hands were the devil's workshop. One thing he needed was a hat; his face and ears had gotten very cold the night before, and the only thing he had to work with was the fresh coonskin. He unrolled it next to the fire, spread it out fur side down and started scraping away any bits of flesh that remained attached to the skin. For it to tan properly, he should have kept the brains, but last night, the only thing he could think of was food and warmth. He knew that if he dried and smoked the skin carefully that it would still be useful and make a warm winter cap. He spent the next couple of hours working on the fur, while trying not to think about the meat still wrapped in his canvas bag. He eventually removed all of the remaining flesh, leaving only the clean, pliant hide with the fur attached. In the meantime, his fuel supply had dwindled down to almost nothing. He decided he had best go outside and gather some more wood before it got dark.

He got his axe and crawled back through the hole to the outside. It was still snowing, but had lightened up considerably. The snowflakes were smaller and the wind had almost quit blowing. The clouds had thinned enough that some sunlight was filtering through to brighten the white forest. Black tree trunks stood out in stark relief. Tree limbs bowed close to the ground with their heavy burden of snow. The snow muted most of the ground features; they showed only as white humps in the snow. The snow covering was unmarred, as none of the forest creatures had yet ventured from their dens. It was a beautiful and eerie sight, as well as cold and scary to a boy who had to fight for survival each day. He almost hated to make the first marks in the unbroken snow, but he knew he must have fuel for his fire.

He started off toward the nearest hump in the snow, hoping that it would be a fallen limb or a dead tree. The first two fallen trees that he found were too big for him to handle; it would have taken considerable chopping to make pieces small enough for him to carry. Finally he got lucky. Using his axe to brush away the snow, he found the top of a good-sized tree that had fallen. He chopped off the extending branches, each bigger than his arm and longer than he was tall. He chopped the wood into pieces, leaving logs about four feet long. He carried the entire tree back a few pieces at a time and slid them through the opening.

Smokey decided that he needed to see what was going on outside and came out to observe the proceedings. The exertion kept David fairly warm, but he often had to stop and place his hands under his arms to warm them. Touching the wet, cold snow with his bare hands chilled them quickly. His boots were getting wet and his feet were starting to freeze. David figured that he had enough wood to last for at least another day, maybe more. There was one more thing he needed. He had noticed some willows growing in a low spot not far away, so he cut several of the long, skinny bushes and carried them back on his last trip. He stopped and got a long drink of water at the trickle coming from the bluff, and crawled back into his snug retreat.

Only a few embers remained of his fire, but he soon had it going again with a handful of dry sticks and leaves. He stacked his wood against one wall, careful to keep the wet, snow-covered logs as far from his bed of dry leaves as possible. When the snow melted, it would leave a wet, soggy spot on the floor. He stacked the wood up standing on end so it would take up as little room as possible in his small space. An area approximately six feet in diameter is big for a tree, but a small space for a boy, a dog, a fire, and a supply of wood. The day had gotten brighter and the snow had stopped by the time David had finished cutting his wood. Now, as the day was ending, the sky was clearing and the sun, low in the sky, was brightly reflecting off the snow.

After David's eyes adjusted to the darkness inside, he could see a small glimmer of light high up inside the hollow tree. That answered the question of why the smoke rose so well from his fire inside the tree. It acted like a giant chimney by drawing air in through the opening in the base of the tree, and the heat rising inside created a perfect draft. David had brought in some of the flat rocks that he had used the night before to cook the 'coon. He arranged them around his fire in the hot coals to use again to warm his supper. Smokey had come inside as well, seeming to know the futility of trying to hunt at this time. He was busy licking the little bit of grease that had remained on one of the rocks. Obviously, he was hungry as well. David took out a piece of coon for each of them. Smokey was happy to get his meal cold, but David placed his portion on one of the rocks to warm up before he ate. He still had a few nuts in his bag, so he took out five or six and cracked them with the flat end of his axe while waiting for his meat to warm.

After eating his meal, he picked up the willows and brought them to the fire. First, he carefully split the bark lengthwise from one end to the other with his small knife, then carefully peeled the bark from the wood. He did this with each piece until all of them were bare. He then separated the inner bark from the outer bark, retaining only the supple and slightly slimy inner bark. He then cut the lengths of inner bark into thinner strips. Taking three strips at a time, he began twisting them together into cords that could be used as rough twine. Once it dried, it would shrink and harden into a tough material for binding things together. He then used the remaining bare sticks to assemble a light framework that would stand over his fire, but be far enough away to keep from igniting. He used the crude twine to tie it all together. The top stood about six feet over his fire.

He took the 'coon skin and, making a round hoop of some willow that was a few inches bigger around than his skin, he attached the skin to the hoop, stretching it across the hoop until it was as tight as he could get it. He made small holes around the edge of the skin with the point of his knife to pass the twine through, which was then wrapped around the hoop. When he was finished, the skin was stretched tight as a drum. He then laid the stretched hide on the top of the rack, directly over the fire, with the skin side down. His small fire would gradually dry and smoke the skin, making it durable and virtually waterproof. The rack could also be used for drying meat if he was able to kill some game.

Once again, he curled up next to the dog and quickly went to sleep.

Chapter Four

It's difficult to tell the time when you're in a room with no windows. Without some sounds to indicate the time, like a rooster crowing or birds singing, there is no natural stimulus to record the passing of time. Smokey seemed to possess some way of knowing that morning had arrived. Once again he was up and licking David's face to wake him. Possibly Smokey could hear or sense something inside the dark tree that David could not, or maybe it was just his bladder. Either way, Smokey had to wake David to get outside because of the sticks of firewood piled over the opening.

David roused and rubbed the sleep from his eyes, and realized that his bladder was complaining as well. He removed the sticks and observed bright sunlight streaming through the opening. Smokey pushed on by to get outside first and David quickly followed. The sun was well above the horizon; David calculated the time to be about eight o'clock. Though the sun was shining brightly, it was still very cold. No snow was melting, but the bright sun gave some promise that it might soon warm up above freezing.

One thing David noticed was that unlike the day before, there were animal tracks in the snow. Squirrels and rabbits had been moving about.

The rabbits were better equipped for snow with their wide back feet, and didn't sink in very deep. The squirrels, however, stayed mostly on the tree branches, only coming down to dig holes in the snow, looking for buried acorns or other nuts. The wind had blown most of the snow from the branches and allowed them easier access to the buds that they loved to eat. David could see several squirrels moving around in the treetops. Rabbit tracks were everywhere, seeming to weave around haphazardly.

David was excited. He was sure he could track down some rabbits and get close enough to kill them with his sling. He decided to eat something first then start tracking. The idea of more 'coon for breakfast didn't sound very good, but it was better than nothing. He got a drink of water and crawled back inside to try to get his fire revived before all of the embers died. There was not much life left in the fire, but he managed to find a few small glowing coals and coax them back to life. He laid a piece of meat on the stone to heat up, and gave Smokey a piece to gulp down. The dog even crunched up the small bones and ate them as well. David didn't take long to eat his either, just letting it get warm enough to take off the chill. He was in a hurry to get going.

It took very little to get ready. He checked his sling, putting his hand through the loop of one string and tightening it around his wrist. The other string he held between the thumb and forefinger of the same hand. He put a rock in the pouch and gave it a couple of twirls; it felt natural and gave him confidence. He wanted to take his axe. Often rabbits would hole up in hollow logs; you could chop a hole in the log and catch them. He finally used some of the crude twine he had made the night before to make a sling to hold the axe so both hands would be free.

Carrying all of the possessions that he had started his journey with, he was ready for the hunt. He left a small fire smoldering under his drying rack and the coonskin curing over the smoke. He knew that he couldn't be gone very long; without adequate clothing, he would probably freeze in a few hours. He had to backtrack the way he had come in to his hidden little garden spot. The area between the bluff and the stream was too small to contain much game. Only squirrels and birds could easily get in or out of the confined area created by the bluff and the steep river bank.

He crawled back through the opening under the rock, getting wet and cold in the process. He brushed the snow from his clothes and hurried so as to generate body heat. The sun was helping, and what little breeze there was seemed to be coming from the south, an indication that it might warm up enough to melt some of the snow. As he proceeded further downstream, he saw more game tracks. The snow was almost knee-deep and Smokey didn't seem to like having to travel in it.

David soon found a set of rabbit tracks that seemed to be very fresh and easy to follow. He began to follow them and found that a rabbit, even in fresh snow, is anything but easy to follow. Smokey was sniffing along behind, but seemed content to let David take the lead on the trail. The track meandered through the thickest of brambles, sometimes going places that David couldn't follow. Finally, he reached a large thicket that seemed impenetrable by humans. Smokey was starting to get excited. Wagging his tail furiously, he plunged on into the thicket. David, expecting the rabbit to come running from the thicket, got his sling ready.

Suddenly, Smokey gave a yelp and took off. Bushes were shaking and the dog was moving as fast as he could. Suddenly, a flash of brown flew from the thicket; there was no chance for a shot with his sling. David watched helplessly as the rabbit easily outdistanced the dog to disappear. Smokey continued the chase, giving an occasional yelp, mostly of frustration, as he plowed through the deep snow. The rabbit could run much faster; his large fur-covered feet and lighter weight kept him from sinking into the snow. David stood still, knowing that the nature of rabbits was to run in a circle. Quite often, the rabbit would return in a large circle to the place where it was jumped. Not this rabbit; he seemed much too experienced for that. Suddenly Smokey's, bark changed. David hurried off through the snow, hoping the rabbit had gone into a hollow log, not a hole.

When he reached the frenzied dog, it was digging furiously at the base of a small hollow black-gum tree. The rabbit had obviously entered the hollow base of the tree and climbed up into the interior of the tree. Smokey calmed down and lay on the ground with his nose as far into the opening as he could stick it. David thought for a minute that he could chop down the tree. Possibly he could build a fire and smoke it out, but first he thought he would try to twitch it out of the tree. He had seen this done a few times, and if the rabbit was not too far up the tree, it could work very easily. He looked around until he found a slender willow sapling that was only an inch thick at the base. He cut it off to about six feet in length and trimmed off all the branches, making it smooth so it could easily be slid up into the opening of the tree. He then split the slender, small end of the stick about two inches back from the end.

He pushed Smokey out of the way and slid the supple stick up into the tree. With about two-thirds of the stick up inside the tree, David could feel the rabbit against the end of the stick. The rabbit kicked and bit at the stick, but to no avail. David pressed the end of the stick firmly against the rabbit and began twisting the stick slowly around and around. The split end of the stick caught firmly in the rabbit's long fur and twisted up tightly. When David felt that it was tight enough to hold, he gently began to pull and apply pressure on the struggling rabbit. As the rabbit tired, he gradually gave up ground and was pulled down into the opening until David could reach its back legs.[9] With a sudden jerk he pulled the rabbit from the tree and swung it in an arc, hitting its head solidly against the tree. The rabbit went limp, immediately dead.

David felt a twinge of remorse as he dispatched the rabbit. Rabbits were cute and he didn't like to have to kill anything, but they were also tasty and he was about out of food. He had grown up knowing that in order to survive, there were many unpleasant tasks that had to be done. David thoroughly enjoyed the excitement of the hunt, but always felt sorry for the creature that met its end so he could survive. He had talked to his Dad about that once, just a few weeks past. His dad had explained that he was very proud of David that he felt remorse, that he too felt the same way and always dreaded having to make the kill when they butchered an animal. Particularly one of the hogs they had raised. He had told him to always be careful around men who felt no remorse about killing. He felt that those men were missing a part of humanity that separated men from animals. David could not think of his folks without becoming very melancholy, and he shook his head to clear his thoughts. It was time to get back to the business at hand.

David's feet and legs were wet and very cold. Now that the excitement of the hunt was past, he noticed the cold ache of his wet feet. The temperature had warmed well above freezing and the snow was melting, making it very wet and heavy. The snow still left on the tree branches was melting and dripping almost like big, cold raindrops. Smokey was looking hungrily at the rabbit, so David carefully eviscerated it and gave the still-warm entrails to the dog. Temporarily satisfied, he trotted off toward the river and the dense thickets that sheltered more game. David followed along behind, hoping the activity would help to warm his aching feet.

David carried his twitching stick, in case it might be needed again, but kept his sling in his right hand, just in case he should see a likely target. As they approached the thickets, Smokey once again started trying to work out the maze of trails and locate another rabbit. David slogged through, looking for a place to get out of the snow and allow his feet to warm up a little. The sun was very warm and there might be a place along the river where a flat rock was exposed, or maybe a gravel bar.

He came to the edge of the river further downstream than he had been before and discovered a large, still hole of water that looked deep. There was a riffle a little ways downstream that indicated a shallow place where he might cross. The bank was only a couple of feet high at this point, and he saw a game trail going down the bank toward the riffle. He moved closer to the game trail and saw that the trail had been made by a small herd of deer that had recently passed through and had crossed the river at the riffle. He could see the tracks going up the bank on the far side. There were several big rocks, almost like stepping stones, that stuck up from the shallow water of the riffle. The steam was very clear and had a gravel- and rock-covered bottom. He walked up to the riffle wishing for a rifle so he could hunt deer and larger game.

Suddenly, there was the splashing of water and the cry of excited ducks, as a flock of startled wood ducks started to take off just below the riffle. David dropped his twitching stick and unfurled his sling that was ready in his right hand. He only had time for a couple of swings around his head before the compact flock of ducks was directly in front of him. Some of the slower ones were still striding on top of the water with their flat feet as they beat their wings furiously to get lift. He released his egg-sized rock at the center of the flock, having no time to concentrate on a single bird. To his delight, he was rewarded with the sound of the rock striking a soft body and one duck dropped into the water and skidded to a stop, where it flopped and floundered.

David forgot his wet, cold feet and raced into the riffle to grab the struggling bird before it could regain its equilibrium. He grabbed the beautiful bird by the neck and whirled the body in a circle, breaking its neck and stopping the struggle.[10] He suddenly realized that he was standing in water nearly waist deep. He would have to get dry and warm as quickly as possible. He found a spot of gravel at the edge of the stream that was devoid of snow, and stopped to wring out his pant legs as best he could. His boots were now full of water, so he sat down and removed them, poured out the water, and rubbed his numb and red feet vigorously to dry them and restore a little circulation. He succeeded in restoring enough circulation to make his feet feel like someone was sticking him with needles. He knew that he needed to hurry or he was in trouble.

He was about a half-mile downstream from his tree. Picking up his game and the rest of his possessions, he set off for the tree as fast as his numb feet would allow. Smokey was still off looking for another rabbit, but he would come back when he was ready. David was hot on top and cold on the bottom when he got back to the tree. He was nearly sobbing with pain as he crawled through the opening, praying that there would be a few embers left for starting a fire. He was not sure that he could concentrate enough to light one from a spark. To his immense relief, there were a few tiny embers still glowing in the ashes. In a few minutes, he had a blaze glowing and was stripped naked, sitting by the fire rubbing his feet and legs. He had placed his wet clothes on the drying rack and was still shivering and rubbing his feet when darkness fell at the end of the short winter day.

It seemed he would never get warm again, but eventually he quit shaking and started to think about how hungry he was. He skinned both the rabbit and the duck, careful to keep the rabbit pelt intact. That was not an easy feat, for the tender skin tore as easily as paper. He spitted both animals whole on some green willow sticks and started to turn them slowly over the hot coals. He would have preferred to cook the duck like his mother cooked the pigeons, but going back outside in the cold was not something he wanted to do with his clothes not yet dry.

While he waited for his supper to cook, he checked his coonskin and discovered that it was dry, and stiff as a board. He removed it from the drying hoop and, holding it over his knee, began scraping off any small scraps of dried meat or fat. The duck had been very fatty and there was a lot of yellow fat next to the skin. He collected as much as he could and placed it on a rock that had a slight depression in the top. He then positioned the rock in the edge of the coals so the heat would melt the fat into oil. He continued to work the hide with his hands to make it as supple as possible.

He took a minute to lace the rabbit skin into the hoop that the other skin had dried on, and placed it on the rack. By the time his duck was cooked, he had the oil from the duck fat worked into the skin and it was starting to get soft and supple. He ate half the duck and was starting to feel pretty good about the day's events. His clothes were dry, so he was able to get dressed, except for his boots. He filled them with dry leaves and laid them on the very top of his drying rack. They would need a good oiling when they dried or the leather would crack. He would have to be careful to save all of the fat from any animal he killed, in order to keep his boots as waterproof as possible.

He discovered that by tying the skin of the forelegs on the coonskin to that of the corresponding back leg, he could effectively turn the skin into a cap. With a little careful trimming with his knife, he soon had a cap that fit well, and covered the tops of his ears. Using his small knife as an awl to make a few strategic holes and some scraps of unneeded hide, he soon had his cap completed. The face of the raccoon was in the front and the tail hung down in back. He felt like a real frontiersman.

It was getting late when Smokey finally came crawling through the opening, wet and looking satisfied, with a full belly and blood on his nose. He finished off the pile of duck entrails that David had left for him, then shook himself, sending water droplets flying all over. David was so happy to see him that he couldn't scold him. The dog stretched out by the fire and was soon sleeping soundly. David banked the fire, placed some logs over the opening to the tree, and wearing his new coonskin cap, was soon asleep as well.

Chapter Five

David awoke cold and built the fire back up just as the sun was coming up. After he got the fire going, he went outside to relieve himself, and watched the pink and orange glow of the few clouds as the sun reached the horizon. It was cold, but promised to be another day above freezing. A lot of the snow had melted the day before, and a few bare spots of ground were starting to show on the south sides of trees where the reflected warmth from the trunk of the tree made the ground warmer. The breeze was still from the south, and with a little luck, most of the snow could melt today.

David knew that in order to survive the rest of the winter, he would have to use any nice days wisely. He needed a supply of meat that would last. Small game would not do it; he had to devise a plan for killing some larger animals with his meager skills and equipment. There were lots of deer, but without a rifle, it seemed insurmountable that he could harvest an animal of that size. He would try to make a bow, but that would take a lot of time. He had made toy bows before, and even shot a few small birds and a couple of rabbits. But there was a big difference between a toy bow and one that would be capable of driving an arrow deep into a deer. He wasn't sure he could get close enough to a deer to hit it even if he could make a bow.

Making arrows was another problem. The Indians knew how to make points out of flint, but he had no idea how they did it. Even the Indians preferred metal tips if they could get them. They used any scrap of metal they could find to make more effective tips for their arrows. He had no metal for tips, but decided that he would make a bow anyway; at least it would be another tool that might come in handy.

After a breakfast of warmed-up duck, he went out looking for a small, straight tree that would make a suitable bow. He wanted something like a hickory or an ash, or maybe even an Osage orange. He had heard that Indians preferred that wood, but in the winter, it would be hard to identify and seemed to be rather scarce as well. He could only remember seeing one once and remembered that it had huge, green bumpy fruits that were inedible.

His mother had been excited to bring some of the fruits back home to put in the cabin and cupboards. She had claimed that this strange fruit kept insects away, much like fresh green walnut leaves would. She often brought in crushed walnut leaves in the summer, claiming that the musky odor helped to keep flies and mosquitoes out of the house.

Smokey reluctantly came along. He obviously was not yet hungry, but didn't want to be left behind. David proudly wore his new coonskin cap for the first time, and was pleased to note that keeping his head warm seemed to keep the rest of him warmer as well. He wanted to explore the far side of the river, but was reluctant to get his feet wet again. His boots were not completely dry from the dunking of the day before, and having wet cold feet for a second day in a row was not something that excited him. Possibly he could find a place to cross where a tree had fallen across, or where the stream was shallow enough for stepping stones to be a possibility. He followed the course of the stream to the southeast, staying on bare ground as much as possible. The ground was muddy where bare of leaves or vegetation. The weather had warmed up enough that the snow was fading fast. He was finding nothing but big trees on his side of the river, but he had seen several that looked like they might be the right size on the far side.

Finally, just downstream from where he had killed the duck, he found a logjam that reached almost across the river. There was about six feet of open water that rushed around the end of a pile of logs and brush that had collected, forming a dam of sand and gravel in the last flood. From his elevated side of the bank, it was an easy jump to the far side. Getting back across might not be so easy, since the bank was about four feet higher than the gravel bar that he could leap to. He would worry about that on the way back. He figured that he could cut a couple of small trees with his axe and make a ladder of sorts to cross back.

The wide river bottom on the far side was a thicker growth of cottonwood and sycamore trees, with thickets of willow and cane. The rich, moist soil created the right conditions to grow a variety of lush plants, and from the looks of the number of game trails that tunneled through the thickets, the area was thick with game. David picked a game trail that was well-used and started off into the forest. Smokey found some interesting scent and trotted off into the forest to do his own hunting, as he often did.

Several deer had recently used the trail, and he decided to follow for a ways to get an idea of his surroundings. The ground gradually rose to a flat table of bottom ground that was a few feet higher than the usual spring floods of the river. He could see the hills rising on the far side of the river bottom at least a half mile away. What a great fertile valley for a farm, David thought; the soil was rich and the land plentiful enough for several farms. He was surprised that no one had yet ventured here. He felt sure that the big creek or small river was probably the Buffalo Fork of the White River that his Uncle Darrell had described. The high bluffs and wide, cane-filled bottoms were just as he had described. He figured that he would have to travel downstream for almost a week to reach his uncle's place, located near the mouth of a creek that flowed into the river from the southwest. His uncle had told him the creek was called Richland Creek[11] because of the wide bottom of rich soil. At the mouth of the creek was a small settlement called Woollum, where some folks named Robinson were building a small mill. It was the last settlement located upstream from where the Buffalo Fork joined the White River.

He supposed that if it were not for the fear of Indian attacks, someone would already have settled this far upriver. He shivered a little at the thought; he would have to be careful, particularly if he were unable to travel before spring. According to his uncle, this was a sacred hunting ground to several warlike tribes that frowned on any encroachment by settlers. The forest and thickets were starting to open up into a grassy clearing of several acres. There were indications of forest fires in the past; probably the Indians burned off the area every year to keep the trees back and create a small prairie to attract game, and possibly to open up fields for planting.

There was no indication of a village in the area, no smoke from campfires or any other signs of habitation. He stopped at the edge of the clearing and watched for a while. He felt a little worried and vulnerable and decided to climb a tree, to get a better look before venturing into the clearing. There were several large trees close by. He selected a huge oak with downward sloping limbs as big around as his body and hung down only four or five feet off the ground. He laid down his axe, grabbed a branch, and swung up into the tree. It was easy climbing and soon he was 20 feet up into the tree with a great view of his surroundings.

He soon picked out several small groups of deer feeding around the edge of the clearing. There were a dozen shaggy buffalo contentedly grazing while one cow watched alertly over the group. At the far side of the big clearing was a group of very large deer--it could only be elk. He had never before seen a live elk or buffalo. He had heard numerous stories and had seen the tanned robes made of buffalo hides with the hair attached. His parents had owned one that they used as a bed cover when it was very cold. He had seen the antlers of elk nailed above the door of taverns and barns, but never one as large as the live one he could see from his vantage point high up in the tree.

He was mesmerized by the abundance of game. How badly he needed one of those buffalo robes. One buffalo would supply him with enough meat to feed him all winter if necessary, and a robe to keep him warm. However, calling the moon down from the sky seemed just as attainable. He continued to gaze at the scene and discovered something that made no sense. There was a pile of trees and brush at the far edge that looked out of place. The way some of the trees were laying in the jumble, it almost looked like a building. He would have to further investigate that sight before heading back toward home. He suddenly realized that he now thought of the tree as home.

He started to slowly climb down from the tree and made an interesting discovery. Three deer were now browsing directly under his tree. The deer--a doe and two yearling fawns--were busy nibbling the buds from underbrush, oblivious of his presence. He was above them and they never once looked up, not expecting danger from above. If he had a large rock, he could have dropped it on one of them. An idea began to form; maybe it would be possible to get close enough to a deer to hit it with a bow and arrow after all. He sat in the tree until the deer wandered off, not wanting to spook them by alerting them to his presence.

He climbed down from his perch in the giant oak tree and, still feeling exposed, he decided to work his way around the more open prairie by staying just inside the tree line. The clearing was at least 200 acres in size, but interspersed with clumps of large trees and wild plum thickets. It wasn't a grass-covered field, but a natural prairie or savanna covered with a mixture of tall grasses and the dried stalks of weeds and small bushes like sumac. The deer had been hard to see, even from his vantage point 20 feet up the tree. Anyone with a similar view could easily see him crossing. The edge of the prairie close to the trees was thick with blackberry briars and a tangle of vines and greenbriar that made walking a miserable experience. David had to retreat at least 20 yards into the forest in order to avoid the tangled growth.

As he neared the far side of the valley and the area of interest that had looked like a building, he started seeing the remains of civilization. There appeared the rotted remnants of a split-rail fence at the edge of the clearing. Clearly, someone had kept farm animals inside a small enclosure. There was a pile of rocks that had been stacked up at the corner, indicating that someone had picked them up to make plowing easier. The first building appeared to be a small log barn. Only the lower part of the square structure remained. Most of the roof was gone and the blackened logs that remained were partially burned. Small trees growing inside the walls were already six to eight feet tall, indicating that the barn had burned two or three years prior.

A few yards further toward the steep hill was the skeleton of a small log cabin. It was in similar condition. The remains of a stone fireplace sat at one end of the cabin; the top half of the chimney was knocked away, possibly by the falling roof. David stood between the remains of the two buildings feeling the hair stand up on the back of his neck. This could not have been anything but an Indian attack on a settler's homestead. Curiosity overcame his reluctance and he stepped through the opening in the side of the log structure that had once been the door. A portion of the door still hung on its bottom hinge and the blackened logs rose only as high as his head.

Little remained that was recognizable as human possessions. There were a few pieces remaining that suggested they were parts of rough homemade furniture. A portion of a table and the remains of a couple of benches were in evidence. There were a few broken pieces of stoneware scattered about. A cast iron cook pot still hung from the hook in the fireplace, the only thing intact that he saw. He was surprised that it had been overlooked during a raid. He picked it up by the handle and checked for cracks. It appeared to be complete and useable, needing only a good cleaning. He couldn't pass up that treasure.

He looked around more carefully. A piece of iron rod was sticking out of the ashes at the edge of the hearth; he grabbed it and pulled. It was an iron fire poker with a sharp pointed hook on one end for positioning the hot logs in the fireplace, which could be handy as well. Using the poker to dig, he started raking through the rubble. In just a few minutes, he had located an unbroken bowl, a small cast iron pan and a stoneware jug with only a portion of the spout broken. There were a couple of knives, one with a bone handle that was rusty but salvageable, and another whose handle was completely burned away, leaving only a couple of rivets dangling through holes where the handle had been.

Near the door, he uncovered a charred white bone, then another, and suddenly realized that at least one of the former inhabitants was still there. Looking carefully, he could make out the outline of the skeleton only partially covered by ashes and partially burned wood. The skull was face down at the very entrance of the door. He had walked right over it when he had entered the cabin, without realizing it. He suddenly wanted to be as far from there as possible.

David grabbed up his treasures, and with his hands full, beat a hasty retreat back into the forest. Suddenly, Smokey was there beside him and a little of his panic receded. The presence of the dog helped to calm him, but did not change his resolve to get away from that scary place. David almost had more than he could carry. He had to stop and get better organized, not wanting to leave anything behind. The cook pot was heavy, but by filling it with the smaller items, it made a more compact way of carrying things. He used some of his homemade cord to tie the handle of the cook pot to one end of the poker and the jug and cast iron pans to the other end.

He now had a load that he could carry on his shoulder. It was heavy and the weight pressed the iron poker into the muscles on the top of his shoulder. He had to stop every few minutes to ease his aching muscles. He decided to save a lot of steps and cut across the clearing, rather than circle around through the forest. It was getting late and he wanted to be back to the warm security of his tree before dark. He found a game trail that went the right direction, and turned toward the clearing. When he reached the edge, he could pick out the tree that he had climbed earlier. Using that as a landmark, he headed across the clearing, aiming a few hundred yards to the left of the tree, and he figured, closer to the river. Smokey trotted along in front, turning occasionally to make sure David was still coming.

After several stops to rest his shoulders, David was nearing the edge of the clearing, when suddenly Smokey crouched down and growled. The hair on his neck was standing up and he was obviously ready to fight. David laid down his load and quickly extracted his axe from the loop around his neck. He was scared, having never seen Smokey act this way before. David was only a few steps behind the dog and was prepared for anything. Smokey continued to growl and suddenly charged forward into a thicket. There was a hiss and a blood chilling scream, and a large something was running through the tall grass with Smokey in hot pursuit. A feline creature with a long tail streaked through an opening, momentarily giving David a view of a large mountain lion.[12] David stood shaking with his axe raised to defend himself. Upon reaching the edge of the forest, the big cat leaped easily into a huge oak tree, then proceeded to snarl and hiss at Smokey as he leaped and bayed at the base of the tree.

David, still not over the sudden fright, picked up his bundle and headed toward the river, calling to Smokey to follow. He almost tripped over the freshly killed deer. The big cat had just made a kill and was starting to feed when it was rudely interrupted by their accidental presence. David, already hungry, suddenly realized the possibilities. The deer was very freshly killed, still warm and bleeding. It was a young doe, and the cat had only started to feed on the soft underbelly. All of the meat and most of the skin was intact.

Smokey was keeping the frustrated cat occupied in the big oak tree a couple of hundred yards away. Common sense told David that he had nothing to fear from the mountain lion, as long as it was treed by the dog. He laid down his burden of new possessions and got out his knife, quickly skinning the deer and cutting off one hindquarter and both backstraps. In about 20 minutes, he had the meat bundled up in the skin and was trying to figure how to carry everything. He finally managed to get everything on his back and started for the river as fast as he could go. It was almost dark when the exhausted boy finally reached the river. He was too tired and it was too late to cut trees for a bridge, so he waded across, once again soaking his feet in the cold water. He finally made it to the tree and got everything inside, only to find that his fire had gone out. He was shivering from the cold, and greatly relieved when he finally got a spark to ignite.

It was much later that a tired and scratched-up Smokey limped into the tree. He had taken a few blows from the sharp claws of the enraged cat, but nothing seemed serious. He looked well-fed, so he must have eaten a share of the lion's bounty before coming home as well. David checked the dog's wounds, even though they appeared superficial, and rubbed some of his melted animal fat into the scratches. The dog curled up in his usual spot in the now warm tree cavity, and was soon asleep. David had eaten hugely of the fresh backstrap, and cut up the rest of the meat for cooking and drying. He went to sleep feeling wealthy and well-fed for the first time ever.

Chapter Six

David spent the next few days tanning his deer hide and improving his newfound home. With the addition of his new possessions and storing as much firewood as possible, the space inside the tree was filling up fast. He cut some stout poles and wedged them inside the tree as high above his head as he could reach, building a kind of second story platform for additional storage. He built a ladder to reach it, and left a good-sized hole in the middle, directly above the fire. He brought in additional flat rocks and built a more useable fire pit that made it easier to cook with his newly found pans. He cut three small trees between six and eight inches in diameter and into six-foot lengths to prepare to make a bow. The wood had to dry and season properly before the shaping could begin, and that could take several weeks before they were ready.

The weather remained dry but cold, especially at night. The supply of deer meat gave David a few days' respite from constant foraging, but he knew he had to find and kill another large animal before the next big snow came. The chance of finding another fresh mountain lion kill was very slim and very dangerous as well. He had to figure out a more dependable way to fend for himself. He needed better tools and weapons in order to survive.

He found and cut a hickory sapling that was about two inches in diameter at the base and not much smaller six feet up. He carefully trimmed and smoothed it, then split the big end enough to allow the haft of the knife with the burned handle to be inserted. He was able to secure the blade tightly by reusing the old rivets and by wrapping the split tightly with wet strips of deer skin and letting them dry. He now had an effective spear with an eight-inch blade. If he could only get close enough to a deer, or possibly a buffalo calf, he had the means to dispatch it.

The first morning after his spear was ready, he prepared to leave shortly after sunup. He took his axe and spear, his two knives, and the pouch containing his fire-making tools, as well as some dried deer meat. He also had a length of his homemade twine coiled around his middle, underneath his new deerskin tunic. He had tanned the hide with the hair on and had simply cut out a hole in the middle big enough for his head. With it hanging down in front and back, he had trimmed it on the sides, poked holes in the edges, and then laced it up the sides with leftover strips of hide, leaving holes at the top for his arms. It made an effective jacket, and with the hair inside, it was very warm. With two pairs of pants and his boots now dry, he was very warm and comfortable. His coonskin cap completed his crude wardrobe. He was the best prepared to face the elements that he had been since leaving home. He was feeling a little cocky as he headed out that morning to pursue some larger game.

Smokey trotted along in front, as was his usual position, as they headed out toward the clearing he had discovered a few days before. He was able to jump across the river by jumping from stepping stone to stepping stone without getting his feet wet, and that increased his sense of well-being. Once again, Smokey headed off on his own after discovering a tantalizing scent to follow. David kept to his game plan. He was going to find a tree at the edge of the clearing and wait for a deer or buffalo to come close enough that he could hurl his spear into its side. It wasn't much of a plan, but it was the only one he could think of.

He had brought the twine to hopefully set a couple of deadfall traps if he could find the right place and material to accomplish that task. His twine was strong enough for possible use as a snare for some smaller animals, but it would never hold a deer. He desperately needed to obtain a supply of meat before the winter weather got serious. He didn't know for sure how many days' travel it would take to reach Uncle Darrell, and he couldn't afford to be caught in another storm without adequate food and shelter. He might not be lucky enough to find shelter as good as the hollow sycamore the next time. David could only guess that he had reached the Buffalo River or one of its tributaries. There were no signposts or anyone to ask for directions.

It took over an hour of steady walking to reach the open valley, but finally he arrived at the tree he had climbed the last time he was here. After looking around, he decided that there were better places to be. He scouted the area until he found a well-used game trail that showed fresh and continuous use, then picked out a large oak that had huge limbs situated right over the trail. He was able to climb a smaller tree that grew beside the large oak and finally to get into the limbs of the giant oak. There was a limb that protruded directly over the trail, about 15 feet above the ground. The limb was about two feet thick and forked right over the trail. He was able to find a comfortable place to sit that looked right down on the trail. He hung his pack over a small limb and arranged his meager arsenal. He had brought his sling and a half dozen stones, larger ones than he normally carried. His axe was tied to his pack; it could be handy for butchering any large game. His spear was a heavy hickory shaft with the burned knife blade firmly attached. The wood was still fairly green and uncured and therefore quite heavy for its size. David figured this was an added advantage.

The tree was situated a little too far into the forest for a good view of the valley. However, there were many game trails coming into the opening, and David could only hope that something would use this particular trail. He had a fairly comfortable perch with an upward-growing limb to lean back on while he sat with his feet on the forked limb. He held his crude spear at the ready and kept his sling and an egg-sized rock nearby as well. The time dragged slowly by.

At mid-morning he suddenly realized that there was movement behind him, over his left shoulder and not far away. He only caught a glimpse from the corner of his eye as something moved behind a small, dense thicket. He grasped the spear tightly as his heart began to race, and his breath seemed loud enough to be heard from a great distance. His hands were shaking as he tightened his grip on the spear. Suddenly, something appeared, coming around the thicket and straight toward his tree. A large black bear was heading directly under the limb he was sitting on. David's excitement turned immediately to fear. He had never been so close to a live bear.

The bear stopped directly underneath his feet and only 15 feet below him, then lifted his nose into the air and sniffed as if smelling something he could not identify. David froze and tried desperately to control his breathing; his heart was about to jump from his chest. After sniffing for several minutes, the bear ambled on up the trail. It took several minutes for David to regain his composure. The bear was far too large and ferocious to consider sticking it with his frail spear. He knew that bears could climb trees and was glad this one had shown no inclination to climb the one he was in.

An hour or so later, a large flock of turkeys appeared. David was amazed how suddenly game could appear and how quietly they moved through the forest. The flock started scratching at the leaves underneath David's perch and seemed totally oblivious to his presence. He decided to try to kill one, and waited patiently for one to position itself directly underneath his perch. Finally, a fat hen scratched and pecked her way into his target area. He aimed carefully between his knees and threw the spear with all his might at the blue-headed turkey. The spear struck the ground seemingly underneath the turkey, but she jumped and exploded into the air. The entire flock followed suit, and with a tremendous effort of wildly beating wings that flailed the air and sounded like a hundred people beating rugs, the panicked flock took flight. Some flew up into surrounding trees while others flew into the open prairie. David almost fell out of the tree with excitement and disappointment.

David had to climb down from the tree to retrieve his spear, and decided that since he was on the ground, he would muster up the courage to visit the burned out homestead once more to look for useful items. He approached the barn this time, dreading seeing the bones lying inside the cabin. The barn was more crudely built than the cabin; there was no chinking between the logs. The building was divided into two compartments, one for animal shelter and one for storage. Most of the froe split shake roof was gone, but it was partly intact over the storage area. A door hung on one hinge partially covering the opening, but swung easily away to allow him to step inside. There was little there; a bucksaw hung on a spike and there were a few rat-gnawed pieces of leather harness hanging on the wall. There was also a large knife, probably made from the remains of a broken crosscut saw blade, hanging there as well. The blade was over two feet long and hafted with a large wooden handle. Although a little rusty, it was still very sharp. A knife like that was used to cut corn stalks for shocking or to clear the wild cane[13] that grew everywhere. The knife and the saw would be very handy items to have, so David picked them up and started back the way he had come. Maybe he would come back later and look around for more useful items, but for now, he had all that he could carry.

The sun was now well past its zenith, so David started back toward his tree home, hoping to arrive before dark. Suddenly, Smokey showed up, wagging his tail in greeting, looking well-fed and quite proud of himself. Obviously he had been more successful than David in his quest for food. As David approached the stream, it was getting rather late in the afternoon and the sun was only a finger's width above the range of mountains to the west. David stopped on the bank just below the logjam, trying to decide how to cross without getting wet. As he gazed down into the water, he realized that there was a fish swimming just below his feet. The water was crystal clear and probably five or six feet deep, but he could plainly see a large fish lying beside a submerged log directly below him. He carefully laid down everything he was carrying but his spear and, kneeling down, he slowly inserted the tip of his spear into the water and gently moved it toward the fish. The light-bending quality of the water distorted his view, but he tried to compensate for that as best he could, and eased the spear closer to the cold, sluggish fish. When he calculated that the tip off the blade was about two feet from the fish, he thrust the spear with all his strength. He felt the blade penetrate the fish and on into the gravely bottom of the stream. Applying all of his weight, he held the spear firmly in the ground until the fish stopped struggling, and then carefully retrieved the spear, being very careful not to dislodge the fish.

When the fish reached the surface, David reached down with his left hand and grasped it by the gills, pulling it and the spear safely up to the bank.[14] It was a large catfish, a mottled brown when seen out of the water, with a flat, ugly head and a long whisker at each corner of its mouth. The fish weighed more than five pounds and would make a fine evening meal. David picked up all of his gear and, carrying the fish by stringing some of his twine through the gills, once again waded across the stream and headed for his tree.

Chapter Seven

The next several days were cold and windy; food was scarce, as game was hard to find. David and Smokey were able to catch just enough to survive, but never enough to build up extra food for travel. When not hunting for food, David spent his time improving his living area inside the tree and working on his bow. He fashioned a fish trap from willow and was occasionally able to catch a fish or two. He also prepared several deadfalls from large fallen limbs weighted with rocks. He fashioned simple trigger mechanisms and baited the traps with fish guts, since Smokey would not touch fish unless it was cooked and he was very hungry.

David worried that Smokey would get killed by one of his traps, but the dog seemed to have no interest in the bait being used. David caught something almost every day. Several 'coons, a mink, two 'possums, and one weasel fell prey to his traps. Except for the 'coons and 'possums, the eating wasn't much good, but it kept them fed. The furs added to David's wardrobe. He stitched the coonskins together and made a warm blanket. The 'possum hides were soaked in wet ashes until the hair came loose, then were smoked, softened, and made into leggings. The mink became a very good hand warmer when turned inside out, and the little weasel became a small pouch.

The bucksaw and corn knife that David had found became very useful. The saw made quick work of cutting firewood into manageable lengths. He was able to complete the loft he had started for more storage, and found that it was sturdy enough to support his weight. He found that by standing on the poles of his loft, he could see through a knothole that allowed him to look across the river. The knothole was one of several that allowed smoke to escape from the tree cavity. Having several exit points for smoke allowed it to be diffused, and therefore, less noticeable. David finally felt that the wood was dry enough to start working on his bow. Keeping it hanging over the fire had seasoned it quickly.

David used the large corn knife as a drawknife, and carefully worked the small hickory pole into a straight, long bow that was nearly as tall as he. He was careful to make the limbs the same length and the same thickness. It was hard, tedious work. He had cut several cane stalks and had about a dozen hanging over the fire drying, from which he planned to make arrows. The bowstring was going to be the hardest component to make as his bark twine was too coarse and stiff. He considered all of his materials at hand as he carefully worked on the bow.

After several days of careful painstaking work, he was ready to try to string the bow. He twisted a couple of strands of dried 'possum hide together, and carefully looped them around the notches he had made on the ends of the limbs. It seemed to work well and he was elated. With a little more scraping on one of the limbs, he was able to draw the bow, and the limbs bent equally. It took all of his effort to draw the bow to the full length of his arm. Sweat popped out on his forehead and the strain made his arm quiver. He could only hold it at full draw for a few seconds. With the bow complete, his next project was the arrows. He measured the length of the arrow by holding one of the cane shafts at full draw and marking the shaft about three inches longer. He then cut all 12 arrows to the same length and made a notch on the small end to grip the string. He carefully smoothed the shaft by sanding off the joint knuckles with a small sandstone rock from the river bed. Two shallow grooves were cut about two inches below the nock point and some turkey tail feathers were split in half down the vein and stuck in the groove with a little pine sap and then the ends were wrapped with wet sinew. Arrow tips were carved from the shoulder bone of the deer killed by the mountain lion. He split the fore end of the arrow and inserted his crude bone points and wrapped the joint tightly with wet sinew. He only had four carved points. He inserted round wooden points into the hollow ends of four more arrows to use for practice or possibly small game if any of the arrows survived his practice.

The following day was warmer and sunny, with only a light breeze from the south. David had found a mud bank to use as a practice target. He hoped it would not damage his arrows too badly. He secured a small scrap of hide in the center of the bank, then counted off 20 paces. After taking careful aim, his first arrow flew well but missed the small target by over two feet low and left. Three of the four arrows seemed to fly well but the fourth wobbled and dived, missing the target by several feet. After adjusting his aim and using only the three arrows that flew well, his shots were getting closer. He never did hit the two-inch piece of leather, but his last four shots were within a hand's width of the target. His confidence was increasing as his aim got better. Tomorrow he would try for a deer.

David hardly slept that night, and was up well before daylight. He strung his bow and carefully checked his arrows. He had not dared test the four bone-tipped arrows, for fear of damaging one of them. He could see no defect. After checking the one that had not flown well the day before, he had determined that the shaft had a slight bend, and one of the feathers that he had used for fletching had been put on a little crooked. Checking his hunting arrows, he could find no similar problems. He had turned his hand warmer into a quiver for his arrows. He placed the four hunting arrows and two of the practice arrows in his quiver and slung it over his head and across his right shoulder. He also decided to carry his spear, in case he needed to finish off a wounded animal.

David left his tree well before sunup. He was a little unhappy when he exited the tree to discover that the warm south wind had brought in low, thick clouds, and the air was damp and foggy. The tree branches, weeds, and grass were wet with the condensed fog. At least the wet leaves would make for quieter travel, allowing him the possibility of slipping into his tree without being discovered by the wary deer. Smokey immediately went off on his own, disappearing into a thicket in search of a rabbit.

The mile-long walk to the edge of the prairie seemed longer than usual because of the darkness. Landmarks were hard to spot, and it took him several minutes of stumbling around in the dark to find the giant oak that he had hunted from before. After finally locating the tree, he tied some twine around his spear and bow, pulling them up into the tree after he climbed up to his favorite branch. It was awkward and noisy getting properly situated. He was hot, wet, and breathing hard when he finally got settled into position in his tree.

The sky finally got a little lighter as daybreak slowly came. Even with the sun rising above the horizon, not much light penetrated the thick clouds. A fine mist was falling and David was getting wet and cold. As he cooled from the exertion, the cold rain began to penetrate his crude clothing and chill him even more. It is hard to sit still when you are wet and cold. But David was determined to stay put until a deer came by.

As he got colder, it was becoming harder to concentrate on his surroundings. Suddenly, there was a doe almost underneath his perch, standing still, looking over her shoulder back down the trail behind her. David was afraid to move for fear of her detecting him above her. He carefully nocked an arrow and leaned forward so he could draw his bow. The angle was bad and he had no room to maneuver his bow into the right position. He slowly rose to his feet, standing on the two large limbs while leaning against the tree trunk to steady himself so he wouldn't lose his balance and fall. This was a lot harder than he had expected. He wished now that he had practiced drawing his bow when he first got into the tree so that he could have worked out these problems before the deer arrived.

Suddenly, the deer made a couple of graceful jumps and then trotted on up the trail, well out of bow range. David's heart sank; he had missed his opportunity. The doe stopped and looked back the way she had come, and David felt sure that she had spotted him. He stood and helplessly watched, wishing for a second chance.

Suddenly, he realized that there was more movement directly underneath and looked down to discover a magnificent buck standing exactly where the doe had been a few seconds before. The buck was much larger than the doe, with a royal crown of antlers adorning his head. David was mesmerized. The huge buck had five points on each beam of his heavy antlers, and a huge neck that was arched like a well-trained saddle horse. He pranced forward a couple of steps and stopped as if offering himself up for sacrifice. David slowly pulled his bow to full draw and was surprised at how easy it was to pull. He aimed carefully at the spot just behind the foreleg and low on the ribs, exactly where his father had always told him to aim.

David released the arrow; to his horror the arrow barely left the bow and impotently struck the ground several feet short of the deer. The deer bolted at the strange noise, but only made a few jumps before stopping and looking back. David looked at his bow and realized that his string had loosened and his bow was totally straight, with the string pressed flat against it. The dried leather had stretched after getting wet and allowed his bow to go slack and useless. David thought he was going to cry. Such a huge deer in exactly the right place and his bow had gone slack. He watched helplessly as the huge buck curiously started coming back toward the tree. The animal slowly walked back to where the arrow lay on the ground and curiously sniffed the strange and unfamiliar item.

David suddenly remembered his spear that was lying across two branches, within easy reach. As the deer sniffed around the arrow, David carefully lifted his spear and threw with all of his strength. He watched in amazement as the point penetrated the side of the deer high on the rib cage and stuck. The deer whirled around and bounded away with the spear stuck in its side. It was soon out of sight, and ran as if it were totally uninjured. David was shaking so badly that he almost fell out of the tree. He finally gained enough composure to climb down from the tree. He retrieved the arrow and tried to decide what to do next. His bow was useless, his spear was gone, and he suddenly felt very vulnerable with only a couple of small knives with which to defend himself. He noticed the blood on the ground and realized that he had wounded the deer severely.

He decided to follow the trail a short distance before heading back. Maybe he could at least retrieve his spear. He easily followed the blood trail; it was plain to see the deer was loosing a lot of blood. His excitement increased the further he followed the wounded animal. After about 100 yards, he found his bloody spear lying on the ground. The blade was slightly bent, but salvageable. The amount of blood increased after he found the spear. It was hard to believe that an animal could lose that much blood and keep on going. Finally the strides of the deer shortened and the amount of blood seemed to dissipate as well.

David almost stepped on the deer before he saw it lying on the ground. The deer had finally given up its life after traveling nearly half a mile into the forest. The boy was elated; he now had a plentiful supply of fresh meat that should last for several days. Plenty for both him and Smokey to make it the rest of the way on down the river to Uncle Darrell's place. He realized suddenly that getting the meat back to his camp was going to be a huge chore. He was one and a half miles from camp with a deer that outweighed him. Even dressed out, the deer was still bigger than he was. He couldn't carry it back in several trips; it would take him two days to move that much meat that far one piece at a time. Part of it would spoil in the rain that was now falling more heavily, or wild animals would finish off what he left before he could retrieve it all. Even if he could carry half at a time, it would mean fifty or sixty pounds each trip and six miles of walking. He decided to dress the deer and see if he could move it after removing the entrails.

Dressing out the deer was hard work. David had watched his dad perform the task many times, but actually making the cuts and doing the work himself was more difficult than he had imagined. He soon discovered that dressing a deer was a lot different than dressing a smaller animal like a 'coon. It took him half an hour to get the chore done. It was still only the middle of the morning, but the weather had gotten worse; the rain was constant and fairly heavy at times, and the wind had switched to the northwest and was cold and gusty. David had carefully saved the liver and kidneys; these delicacies were too important to waste.

Even dressed out, the deer still weighed over 100 pounds. Moving it was going to be hard work. He was tempted to take the time to build a fire and roast some of the liver; he was very hungry. He decided against that possibility. Everything was so wet, it would be difficult to start a fire, and he felt he should not waste the time. He ate a few bites of some smoked meat that he had in his pouch, and decided it was time to begin. The wet leaves helped to slide the heavy animal, but trying to hold the head up by holding on to the antlers was a difficult and exhausting task. After making it only a couple of hundred feet, David was forced to stop to regain his breath. This was going to be a difficult task. Smokey had shown up before he had finished gutting the deer, eaten his fill from the waste, and now walked along in front of David. The dog would stop and wait for David to catch up, then forge on ahead.

After several starts and stops, David collapsed onto the ground to rest and think about a better way to accomplish his task. Meat was too precious and hard to come by to leave some of it to ruin or be eaten by wild animals.

Finally, he remembered seeing his dad bring a big deer home by tying a pole across the antlers and tying the front legs to the pole beside the head. David wasted no time cutting a pole about four feet long and lashing it across the horns of the animal. Once the legs were secured, he grabbed the pole behind his back with both hands and started pulling. The deer slid along behind David on its back a lot easier this way.

It took David the rest of the day to make it back to the river below his tree house. By the time he reached the river, it was almost dark and the temperature had dropped so much that the rain was now mixed with sleet and snow. The river had also risen due to the rain. David decided this was far enough to drag the deer. He quartered out the deer and carried it back to his camp one piece at a time. It took five trips across the swollen river to get all the meat back inside his tree. To say that David was exhausted was an understatement. He hung the meat on the poles of his loft and built a fire. He removed his wet clothing, wrapped up in his coonskin blanket, and immediately went to sleep.

David awoke to Smokey licking his face. The dog wanted to go outside. It was still dark and David had no sense of what time it might be. The fire only glowed, with a few embers having burned down to ash and a few small points of light. As he slowly returned to his senses, David realized it must be very late. He felt around for a few small pieces of kindling to revive the fire. It was cold, very cold. The wind was howling outside with frequent heavy gusts, and the old sycamore creaked and groaned from the stress of the wind against its widespread limbs.

As the fire caught and brought some light, David retrieved his clothes from the drying rack and found that they were mostly dry. He shivered as he shrugged into his cold clothes. Smokey waited impatiently for David to remove the sticks of wood that he used to block the opening. His boots were still soaked, so David opted to make a quick dash outside with bare feet to relieve himself rather than put on the soggy boots. He knelt down to move the wood, and his fingers encountered the cold presence of snow that had blown into the cracks between the sticks of wood. David scraped away some of the snow and Smokey pushed through to the outside.

David decided to retrieve his soggy boots after all before venturing outside. He crawled through the opening and realized that it was past daybreak, but it was snowing so hard that he could see only a few feet. He could see where Smokey had plowed through the snow for a few steps, but the dog was already out of sight. David only took a few steps away from the tree to take care of his bodily needs, and immediately crawled back into his cozy shelter. Smokey followed shortly and then immediately shook himself from head to tail, flinging cold droplets of water all about the shelter. David was extremely thankful that he had been lucky enough to kill the deer the day before. It looked like this storm was going to be much worse that the last one.

David spent the next two days trapped inside while it snowed almost continuously. He only left the warmth of his shelter to take care of bodily functions or to gather wood. The gathering of wood was getting to be more of an effort as he used up the wood closest to his camp.

Chapter Eight

Other than the gathering of wood, the next several days were pleasant. There was plenty of fresh meat for both him and the dog. David stuffed himself; the fresh meat was a luxury. He spent his time drying meat over the fire, tanning the deer hide, and working to improve his camp and his tools. He was very disappointed in his efforts at making a bow. He realized that he needed to make a string that would not stretch when wet. He also started another bow, making it with shorter limbs for easier use in the close confines of a tree. He had no conventional cotton string or hemp and could think of no natural materials that were flexible enough or strong enough to make a string. If he couldn't find something to use, he would only be able to hunt with his bow on days when there was no chance of getting his string wet.

He finally hit on an idea that might work. He ripped the tail from his most threadbare shirt and cut it into narrow strips, then twisted the strip of cloth until it was round and tight. He then took three of these strands and twisted them tightly together and made a loop at each end. He fashioned his new bow from ash, with shorter limbs. The new cotton string was made to the proper length to fit his new bow. It appeared that this might work out.

After completing the bow, he strung it and practiced drawing it to increase his strength and to test the string. Other than a little fraying on the edges, it seemed to work well. He fixed the fraying problem by coating the string with pine sap. He was feeling more confident that this would be a good solution.

David calculated that it must be just about Christmas. He had lost track of the exact number of days that he had been gone, but calculated that the snowstorm had occurred within a day or two of Christmas. He started keeping track of the days by making small notches on a stick. He decided Christmas Day had to have been the day that he killed the deer. At least he was going to call that Christmas Day.

Thinking about Christmas made David very melancholy. Christmas had been sad the last several years, for the previous four, there had only been David and his dad. This Christmas, he was by himself, and unless he found his uncle, it would be that way from now on, or at least until he someday had a family of his own. He certainly hoped that he could survive his present circumstances and someday be part of a family once again.

To stay busy and keep his mind occupied, he made more arrows and also fashioned a long fishing spear with a sharp wooden tip with several barbs notched into the point to keep the fish from pulling loose after being speared. The snow was about two feet deep on average. There were big windblown drifts that were even twice as deep in some places.

The snow melted a bit one day and then froze very hard the following night. A hard crust developed on top of the snow that allowed smaller animals to travel on top without breaking through the crust.

Smokey could mostly stay on top, only occasionally breaking through. The smaller animals and birds were having a rough time getting through the deep crusted snow to reach their food. Rabbits simply ate the bark from trees and bushes above the snow line. Their big feet made travel easy for them. Squirrels managed by eating the buds off of tree limbs and getting at some of the nuts they had cached in hollow trees. Anything on or under the ground was inaccessible to them. Birds like turkey and quail had a very difficult time obtaining food. If the snow lasted very long, a lot of them would starve. Deer had a bad time as well. Obtaining food was not the problem; they browsed on the tender shoots and buds on the end of small bushes and trees. They could even eat the bark of some succulent bushes. The problem was their vulnerability to predators. Their sharp hooves easily broke through the crust of snow, making every step difficult. Most predators like wolves, coyotes, bobcats, and panthers traveled easily on the crust and had no difficulty overtaking the deer.

David found that he was too heavy to walk on the crust. His feet would break through almost every step. In places, it would support his weight, but the next step might allow him to plunge through with the possibility of cutting his legs on the sharp ice or falling and breaking a leg. It remained cold enough even in the middle of the day that the snow didn't melt. David hobbled through the snow to the stand of willows on the river bank and cut enough of the supple wood to fashion some snowshoes. He understood the principal of spreading his weight over a larger area so the snow would support his weight; much like a rabbit's large feet allowed it to hop easily over the surface. It didn't take David long to fashion a crude pair and to his delight they worked very well. They were a little clumsy at first, but he quickly mastered the sliding shuffle that allowed him to cover ground quickly.

It was very cold, but David decided to try hunting for a while; he was anxious to try out his bow. He had been practicing drawing the bow for the last several days to strengthen his arm, and could now hold it at full draw for several seconds. He had continued to improve his winter wardrobe with the skins he had tanned, and felt that he could stay fairly comfortable if he were able to stay dry and keep moving.

David slung his quiver of arrows over his shoulder and got his bag that contained fire-making tools, his knives, and any other assorted items that he felt could come in handy. Picking up his bow, he headed out to make a short hunt. The crust on top of the snow had frozen hard enough to support Smokey fairly well. David followed along on his snowshoes with no difficulty. Getting through the opening between the bluff and the big sycamore was a difficult task that involved taking off the snowshoes and digging snow out of the opening. The snow was cold and dry enough that he didn't get wet, but his hands were aching from the cold when he got to the far side of the passage. He regrouped and headed out, hoping the movement would warm him up quickly. David had made some crude mittens and he had been smart enough not to get them wet removing the snow from the opening to his hideaway.

By the time he got to the river, he was feeling fairly comfortable. The still water above the riffle where he normally crossed was completely frozen over. The entire river was frozen except in areas where the water moved swiftly. He gingerly tried his weight on the frozen surface; the ice seemed to be thick enough and strong enough to support him. Smokey, after sniffing at the edge, trotted confidently across the surface. The snowshoes spread David's weight out enough that he had no trouble crossing. There were lots of tracks in the snow as he got closer to the small prairie. There was one trail that was well-beaten. It was apparent that a small group of buffalo had traveled here recently. Their heavy weight had churned up the snow, breaking through the crust and plowing a trail that several other animals were taking advantage of as well. The buffalo probably had to go to the river for water, finding a riffle that flowed swiftly enough to keep from freezing. They seemed to be using this trail every day, as it was well-trodden.

David followed the trail toward the clearing. He was careful to stay well to one side where the crust was undisturbed and would support his weight. The trail went into a large thicket of pines. The trees were so large, David could not reach around their trunks. They were interspersed with dogwood, redbud, and a myriad of other small understory vegetation. The large pines were far enough apart to allow sunlight to penetrate the canopy in most places, allowing the undergrowth to flourish. In other places, there were small groups of the huge pines that blocked out the sun so completely that no other vegetation could grow.

David saw some movement among the pines and froze. He realized that there were a large number of animals grouped underneath the spreading branches of the pines. He nocked an arrow as he moved slowly forward, making every effort to be silent and keep a large tree directly to his front. Smokey, as always, had gone off on his own to look for game. David crept forward, inches at a time, until he was at the edge of a trampled-down area that seemed to cover a couple of acres underneath the trees. As he peered around the large pine, he could see several buffalo quietly chewing their cud. One old cow was on her feet; the remaining seven or eight were lying on the ground placidly chewing, with steam rising from their bodies and a cloud rising from their nostrils with every exhalation. They were out of arrow shot, even if David had possessed the courage to shoot a fragile arrow into one of the huge beasts.

As David watched mesmerized, several deer browsed around the area, nibbling on the tender tips of the small branches and buds of the understory plants. He noticed a flock of turkeys scratching through the churned-up snow, looking for nuts, roots, or any edible item they could uncover. Several squirrels were also present, digging almost out of sight into the snow to sometimes emerge with a buried nut clasped in their jaws. It was a symbiotic arrangement that nature had created. The heavier animals broke through the snow, allowing the smaller ones access to the ground that they would not have been able to reach on their own because of the frozen crust.

David watched the animals until the chill started to penetrate his boots and make him uncomfortable. Suddenly, he caught a glimpse of another animal off to the side a few yards, and then another. Something large was entering the scene from the outside that was not breaking through the frozen crust of snow. Two wolves were creeping toward the concentration of animals. They were so intent on the game in front of them that they did not notice David. They were even larger than Smokey, but with longer, softer fur. Their dark-colored tails were large, round, and full, and carried at an angle toward the ground. The fur on their back, head, and ears was a reddish-brown, turning to gray on their sides and bellies.[15] David watched intently as they began to stalk the herd of animals with their bellies close to the ground. Their long erect ears were pointed to the front as they concentrated on the animals in front of them.

A small doe was working her way around the edge of the thicket toward David. As his eyes shifted from the wolves to the deer, he realized that there was something wrong with the doe. She was favoring one foreleg, limping with each step. Suddenly, the wolves sprang forward. The doe whirled to escape and nearly fell because of the crippled leg. With precision teamwork, one wolf grabbed a hind leg and the other went for the throat. Within seconds, the deer was on the ground. One wolf had his jaws clamped to the throat and the other was pulling the opposite direction with jaws clamped firmly to the back leg. The struggle was short-lived as the life was quickly choked from the crippled deer.

The wolves began to feed on the warm deer as steam rose from the blood spilled on the ground. The buffalo had all sprung to their feet at the attack, but now solemnly stood watching as if they knew they had nothing to fear. The other deer had run to the far side of the thicket, but had not left the trampled area. The squirrels had quickly scampered up trees, and the turkeys had taken flight to light safely in trees not far away. The wolves paid no attention to the other animals as they quietly ate their fill. David was afraid to move, as he had no idea what the wolves might do if they detected his presence.

Finally, he mustered enough courage to slowly start moving back, careful to keep the big pine between him and the wolves. His first impulse after retreating was to head back to camp as quickly as he could. After a short distance, he realized that he was out of danger and should at least make an effort to obtain fresh meat. With that in mind, he sought another thicket that might hide a similar collection of game animals. He didn't have to travel far, only a half mile or so, until he found another small collection of animals. There were no buffalo this time, but several deer and turkey were using another smaller thicket for protection.

David was once again able to creep carefully to the downwind side of another small yard and stick an arrow into the side of a small yearling button buck that wandered within 30 feet of his hiding place. The deer only ran about 100 yards through the snow before succumbing to the wound. David was jubilant. His first kill with his new bow. This deer was only a third of the size of the previous animal that he had killed. He dressed the deer and pulled it home easily over the frozen snow. He and Smokey would be able to eat well for a few more days.

Chapter Nine

The winter slowly passed by; with David becoming more proficient with his bow, food was easier to obtain. He was able to keep himself fed and add to the collection of skins and furs that kept him warm. He now sported a complete buckskin outfit: britches, shirt, and a new set of serviceable moccasins. His boots were getting a little tight and his clothing that he had left home in was now in tatters. He had even made a few more bowstrings of his threadbare shirts. His hair had gotten long enough that he tied it back with a headband. He looked more and more like a wild Indian.

One day in late February or early March, it started raining. It rained for three solid days and the river turned into a raging torrent. The combination of melting snow and heavy rain filled the river from bank to bank. The once-clear water turned to reddish-brown and swept all kinds of debris swiftly downstream. Large trees were uprooted along the bank, and David was fearful that his tree would succumb to the torrent. Fortunately, David's sycamore was on the higher side of the riverbank and as the water rose, it spilled over the bank on the opposite side and flooded the entire river bottom.

The water rose to within inches of the base of his tree, and David--afraid to sleep inside the tree--shivered underneath a small overhanging bluff until the water started to recede. A warm southern breeze with the smell of spring followed the rain. The tips of the willows turned red and the buds swelled to near bursting on the maples. Tiny leaves appeared on some of the vegetation. Within a week, the river was flowing almost clear, but still higher than its normal level. David went to sleep every night listening to the roar of the water rushing over the shoal just downstream from his tree.

One night, as the warm wind blew gently from the south, the spring peepers, toads, and tree frogs began a cacophony of sound that filled the night with life. Spring had arrived. The sound of life, along with the pleasant roar of the swiftly-flowing water gurgling over rocks sang to him. It was peaceful, and a feeling of contentment washed over him. For the first time since leaving on his journey, David lay next to Smokey and felt at home on the Buffalo. He went to sleep listening to nature's song. The song of the Buffalo.

The next morning, when David stepped outside, he was greeted by a barely apparent green hue in the forest, as long-dormant buds sprang to life. Redbud gave a pink glow to the forest, and wild plum and hawthorn showed their snowy white blooms throughout the forest. Spring is a changeable and fickle season in Arkansas Territory. But for now, it was warm and balmy, with a wonderful sweet smell in the air.

The warm weather was a blessing, and continued with warm southerly breezes and occasional thunderstorms. David and Smokey spent the days hunting and exploring. David was able to recognize some of the new growth as edible greens, and found that he relished the taste of something besides meat. What few nuts he had been able to find early in the season were long gone, and he had subsisted on nothing but meat for the last couple of months. He found a patch of cattail growing in a marshy area not far from the river. The new shoots were tender and succulent, and could be eaten raw or cut up into pieces and added to the stew pot. The tubers could be dug up and peeled like potatoes to add some starch to his diet and a little flavoring added by wild onion bulbs totally changed the flavor of the bland stew he had been eating. He really missed salt; there were times that he craved the taste, even dreaming about it. There was none to be had. He had heard of salt licks used by wild animals and even springs flowing with brackish water, but he had encountered neither.

Now that the weather was moderating, he knew that it wouldn't be long before he could safely head on down the river to find Uncle Darrell's place on Richland Creek. He felt sure he was several days' travel upstream from Woollum. Following along the winding river through the dense growth would be an arduous task. He figured it would probably take him two weeks to journey that far on land. If he had a boat, it would only take three or four days, and he could carry all of his meager belongings. He was reluctant to leave anything behind; he remembered how difficult it had been to survive with the small amount he had carried when he had left last fall.

He planned to leave by the middle of May; that would give him about a month to prepare for the rest of his trip. He was only worried about flooding at this time of year. The river could rise very quickly with the spring thunderstorms. Only a few inches of rain could cause the entire river bottom to be flooded in a few short hours. He figured a raft would be the best way to float down the river, and decided that he would begin work on that the next day. He went to sleep that night with visions of a raft floating leisurely down the river with Smokey and himself sitting comfortably in the middle. Different designs and building techniques wafted through his mind until sleep finally took over.

He awoke late the next morning with Smokey growling and pacing back and forth. The hackles on his back were raised and he was acting very upset. David knew the actions of the dog well enough to realize there was a problem. He sat up and rubbed the sleep from his eyes. It was very dark inside the tree without a fire and his small fire had burned out during the night with only a few embers remaining. He threw a handful of dry grass on the fire for some instant light, and added a few pieces of finely-split pine kindling to get a quick fire going.

Suddenly he heard the sounds that had disturbed Smokey. Human voices were coming from across the river directly opposite his tree. David quickly pulled his fire apart and smothered it with dirt. He didn't want smoke from his fire to give away his position until he knew the identity of the voices. He couldn't understand what they were saying; they were to far away and muffled by the tree. David carefully climbed up on the scaffolding that constituted his attic and peered out through the knothole that allowed him to look across the river. There were four dugout canoes pulled up on the gravel bar directly across from his tree. Several people were moving around and setting up camp, and there was already a small fire going. One man was squatted in front of the fire, possibly preparing to cook some meat. The river was only about 25 yards wide at this location making it easy for David to plainly see what was happening across that short distance. A group of Indians were setting up camp and acting as if they were planning to stay for a while. David realized his danger. If they noticed any indication of his presence, they would quickly find his hiding spot.

For now, they seemed intent on the camp preparations and were not paying much attention to their surroundings. As one prepared food, the others were busy dragging poles and brush from the woods behind them. A small shelter began quickly taking shape right before David's eyes. Four large poles were sunk into holes dug into the soft ground on the riverbank just above the gravel bar. Underbrush was cleared and poles were lashed across the top. The poles in front were about seven feet tall, the ones to the rear about two feet shorter. Next, several long poles were laid across the top, extending all the way to the ground in the rear. Everything was lashed together with lengths of green, supple honeysuckle vine. With several men working, this happened very quickly. There was little talking, everyone seemed to know what to do and completed their various tasks with practiced efficiency.

David counted eight men in the party, ranging in age from a couple of teenagers close to his own age to a couple of old men with long, braided hair that was streaked with gray. They weren't wearing war paint and didn't seem to be acting wary of their surroundings, so David concluded that they must be a hunting party. This was small comfort; they would likely capture him if the opportunity presented itself. There were several tribes that frequented the area. Cherokee, Choctaw, and Osage lay claim to the area, and all three traded freely with white people. Some white settlers had also taken wives from among the various tribes. There were also numerous stories of captives being carried off and never being heard from again. David felt it would be much safer to avoid contact if possible. Since he had no idea which tribe might be represented and what their feelings might be toward lone white boys living in the wilderness, he decided that he had best stay out of sight.

David was really worried; the fact that they were building a shelter indicated that they were going to be there for some time. David knew that some decisions were going to have to be made shortly. He had observed the proceedings for quite some time and it was well into the middle of the morning. His bladder was complaining mightily and Smokey was starting to whine and scratch at the wood stacked over the opening. Finally, to David's relief, the entire group of Indians picked up their weapons and moved off single file into the woods. Two carried muskets and the rest were armed with bows and arrows. As soon as they were out of sight, David tied some of his homemade rope around the dog's neck and removed the covering from the tree's opening. Both he and the dog only made it a few steps before relieving themselves. David took advantage of the absence of the Indians to gather a few supplies. He filled his cooking pot and stone jug with water from the small spring and gathered up what little wood he could still find in the immediate area.

The now-leafed-out willows and other fast growing vegetation along the riverbank blocked him from view of the Indians across the river. He was more worried about Smokey barking and giving away their position. It was obvious that Smokey was disturbed by the presence of the unfamiliar new arrivals. In the distance, toward the prairie that David normally hunted around, he heard the sharp sound of gunfire. Two shots rang out in close succession. The hunting party appeared to be successful. "Well, old dog," said David, "hunting seems a lot easier for them than it does for us. It appears that they will have plenty of fresh meat tonight while we eat jerky. If they stay for very long, that jerky may get mighty old."

Smokey pulled at the rope, wanting to go do some hunting of his own. David figured that his best bet was to stay close to his tree and try to wait them out. Hopefully, their hunt would be quick and successful, and they would only be here a short time. If they didn't find any of his fresh sign or any of his recently set deadfalls, they would have no reason to look for his presence. If they should however, cross the river and come into the small area where he spent most of his time, his presence would be obvious. The steep bank in front of his little compound should prevent a casual reconnoiter.

He decided he should block the small passage under the rock that led to his tree and try covering the sign of his passage. He proceeded to accomplish this as quickly as possible. He had enough food to last several days, as he had been drying and smoking meat for his trip downstream to find his uncle. Yesterday he had picked some cattail and some wild onion and had found a small patch of wild strawberries. He had picked and eaten the few that were ripe, and had planned to go back this morning to look for more. It was the first bite of fruit he had seen since last fall, when he had occasionally found a persimmon that had not fallen from the tree. Strawberries were the first early fruit to ripen.

Suddenly, Smokey growled, looking toward the camp across the river. David pushed the reluctant dog back into the tree and crawled in after him, stopping to quietly block the opening to keep Smokey inside. David climbed back to his observation post through the knothole of the old tree. The Indians were walking up the gravel bar toward their camp, and each was carrying a heavy load. Each carried a buffalo quarter on his back, two of them wrapped in the fresh hide of the same animals. The hindquarters were tremendous loads and the forequarters wrapped in the fresh hides were equally burdensome.

The Indians laid the meat down on the skins and all but two turned around and headed back into the forest. The two older Indians proceeded to start building drying racks and starting fires on the gravel bar. They soon had meat cut into thin strips and hanging over the low fires. It wasn't long before the six who had departed returned with more meat from the buffalo, and a pair of deer as well. All of them pitched in and started tending fires and cutting up meat. It was an interesting sight to behold, and David was fascinated. Had he not been in such a worrisome situation, he would have been thoroughly pleased to watch the intriguing example of everyday Indian life.

The day passed quickly, and when darkness fell, David was hungry for a warm meal. The cooking smells from across the river would mask his own and his fire would be well concealed within the tree. He and Smokey ate well and then ventured outside again for a short time before boarding up the tree and going to sleep for the night.

The next day as David watched, the two older men stayed to tend the meat and the rest left to go hunting. David quickly became bored and tried to find something that he could do quietly to pass the time. He removed the wood from the opening and sat just inside the tree. With the light filtering in, he worked on making more arrows. The day dragged on. Eventually there were shouts across the river. The hunters had returned with more game. They appeared two by two, carrying poles across their shoulders that were heavily laden with turkeys and deer. Two more deer and several turkeys were added to their larder. Most of the afternoon was spent preparing the meat.

Late in the afternoon, there was a splash of water and it seemed that all of them had decided to take a break and bathe naked in the cold water. They swam and played and splashed water, just like David remembered doing the summer before with his father in the clean, cool water of Bull Creek. On hot summer days, after working all day in the fields, he and his father would refresh themselves before returning to the cabin. These were some of David's fondest memories.

David noticed that the two younger members of the party had apparently decided to swim across the river. They were racing and heading toward his tree like a pair of young otter. The roots of the old sycamore hung down into the water on one side, and the action of the moving water had washed the soil from around them, creating a tangle in the water that attracted numerous fish. The boys were headed straight for those roots, which were directly underneath where David peered through the knothole. They arrived at the tree and held onto the roots to rest for a moment from the effort. They laughed and chattered just like any other boy would have done. They were very near David's own age and he wished fervently that he could join them in their sport.

After regaining their breath, they swam back across the river as fast as they could, swimming underwater and popping up occasionally for a quick breath. Smokey had heard the boys, and growled low in his throat with bared teeth and raised hackles. David was a little shaken and crawled down from his perch to quiet the dog. It did not appear that the boys had heard Smokey's growls.

The routine continued for a couple more days. David and the dog would only leave their hideaway during the night or for brief periods during the day if the camp across the river was deserted. Food was starting to get low but the boredom was the worst. Having to stay so quiet and well-hidden all the time was difficult. Smokey could not seem to understand the reason for his confinement. He had never been tied before, and constantly strained at his tether or paced back and forth as far as his rope would allow. David was starting to be concerned about their lack of food. There were only a couple of meals left and the Indians showed no inclination for leaving. They were still busy hunting and preserving meat.

David decided that the following day he would have to either hunt or fish. If he could get started before the Indians were up in the morning and get downstream below the bluff, he should be able to safely hunt the opposite side of the river. The Indians had only hunted the south side, so he should be safe hunting on the north side and well back from the river. He decided that he would take as much of his gear as possible, camping well back in the forest away from the river for a few days until the Indians left their hunting camp.

Trying to decide what to take was a difficult task. He packed his shoulder bag with what little dried meat he had left and all of his small tools, as well as his sling and a few carefully-selected rocks for ammunition. He would, of course, take his axe and his bow with all of his arrows, and his spear that was tipped with the knife blade. His corn knife he carried like a sword, thrust through his belt. There was no way to carry his saw and the heavy cast iron pots and pans that he had salvaged from the burned-out cabin. Also, his many skins would have to be left behind, except for his coonskin blanket that he rolled up and tied with a thong.

At least an hour before daylight, David crawled from the tree, and leading Smokey on a short length of rope made of rawhide, he started out by moonlight.

The moon was about three-quarters full and supplied ample light to follow the now well-known trail. It was only about a quarter of a mile downstream to a small creek that entered the river at the foot of the bluff just below the riffle where David normally crossed the river. David would have to wade across the creek then follow the game trail that lay on the east side of the small stream. He had never scouted very far upstream, but he suspected that its origin was a large spring somewhere above, as the water was very clear and cold. There was also lots of watercress along the edge, and peppermint growing along the bank. David was looking forward to chewing on some of the wild peppermint.

Smokey was not broken to lead and pulled David along, straining at the short leash. They made it to the stream and waded into the icy cold spring water, when Smokey suddenly froze and then growled and lunged forward, pulling David off balance. David fell full-length into the water, but the rawhide leash was looped around his wrist and he managed to hold onto the dog.

David heard surprised voices and arose to find several startled Indians standing on the bank, some with weapons pointed at him and the dog. David froze, forgetting he was cold and wet. Smokey continued to growl and lunge but David was able to hang onto the rope with both hands by dropping his spear and bow. Finally, he soothed Smokey enough to follow the instructions of one of the Indians, who was motioning for him to come out of the water. He was saying something that sounded like "Ho,

Ho," and motioning with his arm. It was apparent that he wanted David out of the water.

A cold and dripping David slowly exited the stream, to be surrounded by the Indians, who were all talking and laughing in an unintelligible tongue. Smokey was still upset, but even he seemed to recognize the futility of further struggle. It was still too dark to clearly see what was going on, but one of the Indians remedied that by quickly starting a fire. Another Indian then splashed into the water and retrieved David's dropped bow and spear. They all looked curiously at the strange weapons and another poked at his bag motioning for him to drop his other things.

David carefully lowered his pack to the ground, then slowly removed the corn knife from his belt and laid it on the ground along with his axe. Holding his hands palm out, he finally found his voice and said, "Peace, I am a friend," over and over again. Someone reached over and removed his sodden coonskin cap and revealed his long blond hair.

"White boy dress like Injun, splash like frog." There was a hoot of laughter following that remark by one of the older men. "Boy say, 'Peace, friend.' Dog disagree." Another chuckle followed. "Maybe dog be more friendly after boiling in pot for day or two."

David sprang between the dog and the Indian. "You leave my dog alone," David nearly sobbed. "He's just tryin' to protect me!"

"No eat dog," replied the Indian, "him too tough, might break tooth." David realized that the Indian was teasing him and relaxed a little. "Where white boy going in middle of night? Boy might run into bad Injun, get scalped." Another round of laughter passed through the group.

"I was just goin' huntin' and I don't mean any harm. If you'll let me go, I'll be on my way, no bother to you."

"We go to camp, wait 'til sun come up, decide whether to scalp you, eat you, or let you go." The old Indian grinned broadly as if he were very funny, and motioned for all to head back to camp. David tugged at Smokey and followed along behind the old man, with the rest of the Indians following along behind in single file. They crossed the mouth of the stream, then the riffle across the river that was only about thigh deep, but swift and hard to keep from being swept over on the slick rocks. They trudged up the gravel bar to the camp, where the boys immediately threw some wood on the fire. David was glad for the warmth, but it was swiftly getting light enough that the fire wasn't necessary to see.

"White boy hungry?" asked the old man. "Sit, eat, talk, we decide what happen to you." Someone handed David a large piece of freshly-cooked meat and pointed to a place on the ground by the fire. David sat down cross-legged and the eight Indians solemnly joined him on the ground in a circle around the small fire. David continued to hold tightly to Smokey's leash. Smokey lay down beside the boy but was as tense as a coiled spring.

David discovered that he was hungry, and tried a bite of the warm and tender meat. He bit off a small bite and tried to feed it to the dog, hoping that would calm him down. Smokey ignored the meat, never taking his eyes off the Indians for even a second.

"Why white boy alone in woods? Where rest of white folks?" asked the old Indian.

Thinking fast, David replied, "The rest of our camp is just upstream from where you found me. My father and the rest of the men will be looking for me shortly."

"We wait here, when they come, we eat big feast and smoke pipe, maybe trade."

David realized he was caught; it sounded like these Indians were friendly and just surprised to find a lone white boy. Sooner or later, he would have to reveal his lie and admit to being alone.

"I'll just eat, then take my dog and go back to camp. I'll tell them where you are camped, and they will come in a day or two to trade."

"Boy eat, then we go to your camp with you and greet white men, make trade."

This was getting worse by the minute. David had hoped they would fall for his ruse and give him a chance to get away. Now they would probably be angry when he told them there were no traders, nor any other white people for that matter.

David stalled for more time, slowly eating the meat and trying to think of a way out of this predicament. He exaggerated his appreciation of the meat, trying overly hard to communicate his friendliness. That was not so hard to do; the meat was very good and he was very hungry.

David was beginning to feel a little ridiculous. The Indians seemed very friendly and were having a good time teasing him. Neither he nor the dog had been harmed in the least. In fact, they were feeding him and treating him as a guest. That might change when they discovered he had lied to them about being part of a trading party. He now regretted lying to them about that. His dad had always told him that it was always better to tell the truth and let the chips fall where they may. He now understood the wisdom of that concept.

The older Indian once again spoke in his broken but easily understandable version of English. "White boy have name? This Injun name Crow." Pointing around the fire, he named the rest of the group. "These two my sons, named in old way, Big Elk and Bull that Roars. Boys belong them, named like white men, Sam Crow and Charley Crow. [16]

"Boys grow up in white man's time, have names like white man. They will talk and live like white man someday. When deer and buffalo gone, they dig in ground, grow beans and 'taters' like white man." The boys obviously understood some English as well and snickered at this last statement. "Boys laugh now, I see white man come before. Soon animals disappear; white man cut trees, dig up ground. Before army moved our people from their homes, we live like white man. They took houses, made us travel long way to new land just for Injun. Now white man come again. Soon be same again. Boys must learn new ways better."

He completed the introductions by naming the three remaining Indians. "Other old Injun brother to my woman. Him called Lone Tree." Pointing again at the remaining two, "Boy belong him called Running Deer, other called Hawk." David assumed he was not related.

David realized that they were waiting for him to give his name. "I am called David, David Christian." David hesitated for a minute and decided to clean up his lying. "I was afraid to tell you that I am alone, there is no trading party. I am traveling downriver to a place called Woollum to meet my uncle. He has a place on Richland Creek near a mill owned by some people named Robinson."

For the first time, someone else spoke. "I know place," said Lone Tree. "Man at mill trade for skins. I go there last fall, trade for powder and shot. Several white men have house near mill. Man called Christian live short walk up creek."

David was elated to hear they knew of his uncle. "How far to Woollum?" he asked.

"In canoe, three, four day. Walk, take long time. Much brush, no trail." David suspected as much, but was disappointed to have his fears verified.

"Where David from?" asked Bull that Roars.

"I come from a place near the James River, north of the White River. I left last fall and spent the winter here after getting caught in a big snowstorm."

The Indians looked around as if expecting to see a cabin that they had overlooked. They seemed unsure whether to believe him or not.

Another listener chimed in. "Where sleep? Build fire?" asked Big Elk.

David had no way out of revealing his secret location; he was trusting everything to this little band of seemingly friendly hunters. David pointed across the river. "In that big sycamore tree," he stated.

The Indians looked from one to another as if in disbelief. After a minute of incredulity, Sam and Jim jumped up and ran to the river and swam across as if in a race. They climbed up the dangling roots of the old tree and disappeared from view behind the willows along the bank. In a few minutes, Sam was standing on the bank in full view holding aloft some of the belongings David had left behind--his bucksaw in one hand and his stone jug in the other. With that, all of the Indians had to go see for themselves. They all, David included, swam across the river and climbed up the roots.

In a matter of minutes, David and all eight Indians were squeezed inside the tree. There was barely enough room to fit, but no one wanted to be left out. The boys, Sam and Charley, climbed atop David's loft and squatted, looking down at his small living quarters. There was much discussion, some in English, some in their own tongue, but they were greatly impressed by David's ingenuity. They were all slapping him on the back and asking him questions faster than he could answer.

The rest of the day was spent on the gravel bar in front of the camp. Sam and Charley were curious about everything David had done. They looked at his bow and arrows and tested the pull of the bow. They ended up trying his fish spear and getting enough fish for another feast. They had stuffed the fish with watercress and coated them with clay, then covered them with coals, much like David's mother had prepared the pigeon. When the clay had baked hard, it was cracked and pulled off, taking the scales and skin with it, and leaving the juicy flesh easy to pull from the bones. Hunting was forgotten that day and only a minimal amount of work was done. Smoking fires were tended and a few hides were scraped, but most of the day was spent getting acquainted.

David was happy to have another human being to talk to, and soon forgot the differences in their skin color and became accustomed to their way of speaking. Their lack of understanding about the use of English adjectives was soon unnoticed.

Finally, the day came to an end with them all sitting around the fire, eating the last of the fish.

"David make good Choctaw. Make bow and spear. Hunt for food. Live in forest. Need no help. Much better Injun than white man," said Crow.

David knew that was a compliment and beamed in gratitude.

"Day comes we finish hunt, then dry meat. Few days we leave. Go to village. Boy Who Lives in Tree can make hunt then travel with us to village. Richland Creek, not far from village."

"I would be happy to hunt with you tomorrow, and if you have room for me and my dog, we would travel with you to your village."

Smokey had calmed down considerably, but was careful to stay as far away as he could while still seeing David. He had not left to go hunt alone as he usually did, but stayed in sight of David at all times.

The matter of hunting the following day seemed to be settled, and everyone got up and stretched and started getting ready for bed. The boys, Sam and Charley, offered to take David across the river in a canoe. Smokey refused to come, but trotted off down the river toward the place where they usually crossed.

Chapter Ten

The night went by slowly for David. Charley and Sam had been slow to depart. They had carefully looked over all of his possessions and seemed in awe of David's living arrangements. With a mixture of English, Choctaw, and sign language, they asked question after question about David's experiences. They were very impressed with his story of taking the mountain lion's kill and also the story about killing the deer with his spear. They were all quickly learning new words and signs in each other's language. Communication, at first awkward, improved rapidly.

Reluctantly the boys departed for the night, leaving David to contemplate the day's happenings. It was great to have some friends. David was already feeling comfortable with the Indians. For the first time in a long time, David went to sleep not feeling alone. He didn't even cover the opening of the tree before going to sleep. Smokey would not come inside the tree while the Indians were there. After they left, he finally came in and curled up in his usual place.

David awoke to the sounds of Smokey growling and a tapping on his tree. He was startled to hear a voice say, "Time to hunt. Come quick."

It took David a moment to gather his wits, but he realized it was Sam waking him for the morning hunt. He threw some dry grass on the remains of his fire and was rewarded with an almost instant fire and light enough to see a grinning face peering through the opening of his tree. "Come on in while I get ready," he said to Sam, who was quickly followed through the opening by a grinning Charley as well. David had slept with his clothes on, so it did not take him long to lace up his moccasins and start gathering up his weapons.

"Should I take my spear as well as my bow?" he asked.

"Arrows seem small for bear, maybe take spear. Run up close, stick bear good, run away fast," replied Jim.

David couldn't tell if he was teasing or not. "Are we really hunting bear today?" he asked.

"Got plenty dried meat, need bear grease. Get bear grease, we go home few days," answered Sam.

"I've never hunted bear before. How do we do it?" David asked.

"Bear very hungry in spring. Look for things bear like to eat, find bear. Sneak up close, shoot bear," Sam answered with a shrug, as if to imply that everybody knows that.

David decided to take his bow, his spear, and his axe, just in case the bear got too close. He didn't relish the idea of getting close enough to a bear to use any of these items, but he thought he should take them all just in case.

Now that it was warm, David wore a pair of his home-spun pants that were getting too short, and a sleeveless deerskin tunic. It was warm for a fur hat, so he only wore a headband to keep the hair out of his eyes.

Except for his blue eyes, he would have passed for an Indian. In fact, the Indians were dressed more like white men than he was.

David wasted little time with his morning routine and quickly exited the tree with his hunting equipment. He got a drink of water and followed the boys down the same trail he had taken the day before. Smokey followed along, seemingly unsure and somewhat suspicious of the whole thing. They joined up with the rest of the group at the same place he had encountered them the day before. This time, he crossed the creek and fell in behind the group as they quietly hurried along the trail, making almost no sound. Sam and Charley followed closely behind him.

After a half hour of swift travel, they suddenly stopped just as it was finally getting light enough to see individual trees. They seemed to be at the edge of a large clearing that spread out along the creek. The grass and low, thick vegetation was glistening with dew as the pink glow of the imminent sunrise lit up the little valley. They had turned away from the creek and climbed a hill, and now looked down on the valley from a bluff above the creek. A fire had obviously burned across the valley the previous fall. The remaining trees had blackened and scarred trunks. A few dead trees stood dark and solitary as sentinels watching over the valley. The opening was lush with grass and new vegetation springing up from the roots that were unaffected by the fire. New shoots of wild cane, numerous wildflowers, the distinctive umbrellas of mayflower, lambs-quarter, as well as new suckers coming up from the roots of burned trees, created a lush browse for many animals.

As the sun rose above the pink horizon, the dew glistened like a sea of diamonds. It was a beautiful sight. As the light improved, David could make out dark shapes moving slowly through the knee-high vegetation.

A small group of elk stood quietly in the middle of the valley--two cows with young calves. One calf was hungrily suckling, his short tail twitching rapidly from side to side. A flock of turkeys was not far from the creek. Two large gobblers were strutting with tails fanned and wings extended. Their feathers were fluffed up, making them appear as big as a bear, as they tried to impress the blue-headed hens and young jakes that pecked and scratched around them.

Suddenly, Lone Tree pointed toward the north and all eyes followed his finger to a large black hump that stood above the glistening vegetation. David could hear the gobble of the tom turkeys below them, but the sight of the bear feeding only a few hundred yards away made everything else disappear from his focus. Lone Tree, who had one of the two old rifles in the group, and Bull That Roars, who possessed the other, whispered quietly for a few seconds, then quietly eased back from the bluff and silently slipped away into the thicker forest. The rest of the hunters waited quietly and watched the bear as he slowly grazed across the field, occasionally lifting his nose high into the air to check his surroundings.

Bears have very keen noses and acute hearing, but have very poor eyesight. The wind was from the south and the bear was quartering across the large clearing from northwest to southeast. He continually tested the breeze to check for danger to his front, but had to depend on his ears to warn him of danger to his rear.

Suddenly the two stalkers appeared in the stream bed, slowly and carefully working their way upstream to get up wind of the bear. The stream was about four feet lower than the surrounding field, so by crouching down low, they were able to slip along below the angle of sight of the bear. A gully entered the stream from the field and gave the two hunters an opportunity to enter the field out of sight of the bear and upwind of his position. They were soon out of sight, crawling up the gully that angled toward the bear. David found himself holding his breath as the excitement built. No one spoke, not even a whisper. Everyone kept their eyes locked intently on the bear grazing in the field.

After what seemed an eternity, there was a puff of smoke about 50 yards to the north of the bear, followed by the sharp report of a rifle shot. The bear jumped and took off in a dead run, seemingly unhurt. David was amazed at how swiftly the bear crossed the opening and disappeared into the forest on the other side of the clearing. Lone Elk and Bull That Roars appeared at the place where the bear had been when the shot was fired, and started following its trail through the wet grass. David had been holding tightly to Smokey through the entire ordeal, but as everyone arose to go help with tracking the bear, Smokey could not be contained. He jerked free, breaking the leash, and took off at a dead run.

Everyone ran to help trail the bear. Smokey won the race. As he got to the bear's trail, he bayed and took off in pursuit, baying loudly every few jumps. He soon passed Lone Elk and Bull That Roars, and ran baying into the distance. Everyone joined up on the far side of the clearing, and Lone Elk pointed to a few bright red spots of blood showing in the trail. The bear was wounded and Smokey was hot on his trail. The Indians had never hunted bear with a dog and seemed angry that Smokey was chasing the bear. David was only worried that he might catch him. He would not be a match for an angry 500-pound bear.

"Dog chase bear to Big Muddy River. Too far, never see bear again," Lone Elk said with disgust. "Make grease outta' him, no chase bear next time."

"Wait," David begged. "He will tell us where the bear goes. We can follow and find the bear. Just listen, you can tell when he trees the bear, then we can walk up and shoot the bear out of the tree. My father used Smokey to run bears all the time. He is one of the best bear dogs in the country."

"Listen. He has stopped running already, he has the bear treed." The dog's trailing yelps had changed to a frenzied barking.

Everyone started off in a trot, following the sound of the dog. He was a good half mile away and the terrain was rugged, but in a few minutes they were close enough to hear the roar of the angry bear as he tried in vain to grab the dog that was tormenting him. He had not climbed a tree, but instead he had backed up to a bluff and was trying to grab the dog that barked and danced just out of his reach every time he swung a massive paw at the dog. One blow from the clawed paw would have killed Smokey instantly.

The hunters cautiously approached the melee; the two armed with guns carefully checked their priming, not wanting a misfire. Bull That Roars and Lone Elk advanced to the front of the party and moved to within 20 yards of cornered bear. Bull That Roars raised his gun and tried to take careful aim at the bear as it lunged at the dog. He fired, and the bear roared with pain and rage and turned toward his new attackers. The bear immediately charged the group of hunters. Lone Elk fired his gun and the bullet connected but the bear didn't slow. The angry bear roared with rage and a bloody froth dripped from his mouth as he charged. A couple of the hunters loosed arrows at the bear before turning to run. The rest quickly started climbing trees. David froze; the bear was coming straight for him. One more jump and the bear would have been right on top of him, but

Smokey grabbed the bear by one hind leg and caused the bear to stop and whirl toward this latest attack. He caught the brave dog and knocked him loose, then lunged again for the injured dog.

David could not watch his faithful companion get mauled by the enraged bear without trying to save him. He dropped everything but his axe and ran to Smokey's aid. He got there just as the bear grabbed the dog with his teeth. The bear had the dog by the loose skin at the back of his neck. David swung his axe and buried the blade deeply between the bear's ears. The bear fell lifeless, his head resting on Smokey. David pulled the injured dog away from the dead bear and cradled his head on his lap. The dog was bloody, and four deep, parallel gashes lay along his right side. The skin of his neck was ripped and torn. Smokey lay there, licking the tears from David's face as he held the bleeding dog in his arms.

The Indians quietly gathered around the gruesome scene. Crow broke the silence by quietly speaking to Lone Elk and Hawk in their own tongue. They immediately trotted off. Crow knelt down by the badly torn dog and began inspecting his wounds.

"Dog very brave. Great warrior. His hide much tough. Dog not fight bear, some of us be on other side talking to spirits. Boy Who Lives in Tree, great warrior. Kill bear with axe, very brave. Dog need big medicine. Hawk great healer. He make medicine. Fix dog up good."

David felt a slight glimmer of hope that Smokey might survive.

Hawk and Lone Elk both jogged back to the concerned gathering. Lone Elk was carrying a double handful of moss while Hawk carried several strange-looking roots with green stems still attached. David recognized some of the plants. May apple and mullein, along with a plant called rabbit root, were some that he recognized. Several others were unfamiliar. Hawk knelt down by the dog and examined the wounds. He placed one of the roots in his mouth and started chewing. When he had it well masticated, he spit the juice into one of the open wounds and started chewing another root. He reached over and handed a root to David and said, "Boy chew. Make juice. No swallow. Make belly ache if swallow." He spat more juice into the wounds and motioned for David to do the same.

This continued until Hawk concluded that there was enough of the juice in each of the wounds. He then pulled a needle made from the very sharp thorn of a locust tree from his pack. Using thread made from a yucca plant, he stitched the skin together.

David's mouth and tongue were now completely numb. He could bite his tongue and not feel it in the least. He kept trying to spit out all of the bitter-tasting juice so he would not swallow any, but his mouth was not working correctly. It simply drooled down his chin.

Smokey submitted to the sewing without a whimper. David surmised that the wounds were as numb as his mouth.

When the skin was pulled back together, Hawk packed moss over all the wounds and then removed his hunting shirt. Using his knife, he started cutting it into strips. He wound the strips around the dog's torso and tied them tightly to hold the moss in place.

"Dog tough. Maybe live to fight 'nother bear. First time use medicine fix dog, maybe work, maybe not."

David gently laid the dog's head on the ground and walked down to the creek. He cupped his hands together and dipped some of the clear, cold water and carried it back to Smokey. The big dog lapped it up gratefully.

Attention had returned to the bear and everyone gathered around to admire the behemoth. They all claimed it was one of the biggest bears they had ever seen. Hawk removed the axe from the bear's head, then placing his hand on the bear's snout, he started chanting in a monotone voice as he held his other hand toward the sky. When he finished the chant, he dipped his fingers in the fresh blood and walked to David. He placed one hand on David's head and motioned to the four directions with his bloody hand while he chanted some more. Upon finishing that chant, he placed his bloody fingers on David's forehead and drew four bloody streaks down his face. Everyone whooped at the completion of the ceremony and immediately started to butcher the bear.

David was bewildered; he knew something important had just happened, but not understanding Choctaw, he had no idea what had just transpired.

Charley helped him out. "Hawk thanked spirit of bear for sacrifice of his life. Ask he forgive us. We need bear to survive. Someday our bodies be used make things grow. Help others survive. Killing bear made you Choctaw warrior. His blood placed on face so bear will recognize you in next life. Help you after you cross to the spirit world. Your Indian name is now Boy Who Lives in Tree and Slays Bear."

David was still in a state of shock and wasn't exactly sure what it really meant to be a Choctaw warrior, but he did try to stand a little taller.

It took two trips to get all of the bear meat and the hide back to camp. They made slings by running two poles through the armholes of their shirts and by placing the meat on the makeshift stretcher. Two men could then carry a very heavy load on their shoulders. On the second trip, they carried Smokey on one of the slings. He lay still with is eyes shut, breathing heavily. He never whimpered or tried to move.

David was sure the dog was dying and he made both trips in a fog, blaming himself for letting Smokey chase the bear in the first place.

The next two days, David cared for the dog night and day. Smokey would occasionally wake up and David would give him water to drink. His nose was dry and hot to the touch. David didn't see how he could survive his terrible wounds.

There was much activity about camp. A second, much smaller bear was killed the following day and everyone was busy. Every pot they had brought was filled with fat and melted over the fire to render bear grease. There was much feasting on the fresh meat, but David ate very little. Hawk checked Smokey's wounds daily, applying fresh moss and retying the bandages wound around his body when it was needed.

On the third day, Smokey got up and limped to the river and lapped up a long drink of the fresh water. He then limped back to his bed that David had made of some of his tanned hides and slept the rest of the day. On the fourth day, he ate a little dried meat, drank more water, and slept some more. On the fifth day, he got up, wagged his tail and ate a good meal before going to the river for a drink. He even gnawed on a bone for a while between naps.

David was beginning to be encouraged that he might live.

On the seventh day, Hawk removed the bandages and inspected the wounds. Using his knife, he carefully cut the stitches and pulled them out. He then rubbed some ointment made of bear grease mixed with ground herbs into the wounds and left them uncovered.

There was another ceremony that night, and Crow placed a necklace made of the huge bear claws around David's neck. Everyone chanted and sang, while Smokey slept through the whole thing. David was starting to understand a few of their words, but not enough to follow much of what was being said.

The next day, the Indians started packing up camp. They had spent better than two weeks camped at this location and had accumulated a large amount of dried meat and animal skins.

Sam and Charley told him that the following morning they would leave in the canoes to float down river to their village. David was worried there would not be enough room in the canoes for him and Smokey.

Chapter Eleven

The next morning, David awoke to Smokey crawling across him to go outside. It was close enough to daylight that he could see the opening of the tree as a lighter hue than the surrounding blackness of the tree. The previous night had been the first night that he and Smokey had spent in the tree since the fight with the bear. He had wanted to spend one more night in the shelter that had become home, before he left for what would probably be the last time.

Sam and Charley had paddled them across the river in a canoe and helped David carefully lift the still stiff and sore Smokey onto the bank. Smokey had happily wagged his tail and limped over to the tree and crawled inside. When David entered and built a small fire, Smokey had curled up to sleep in his favorite pile of leaves, looking very content. As David lay on his mattress of grass and leaves, he listened to the forest come alive outside his tree.

The call of the awakening birds was an overwhelming symphony. David knew some of the more common birds by name, but there were many more that he had no idea what to call them. There were robins and bluebirds, cardinals and finches, several kinds of sparrows that sang different songs. The busy wrens buzzed all over the place, singing with a voice much bigger than their tiny bodies. There were yellow birds, black birds, red, blue, and green birds, gray birds and brown birds, and they all sang a different song. David was sad to leave this wonderful and lonely place that had become his home. He was anxious to see his Uncle Darrell, but leaving here was going to be hard.

David sat up and threw a handful of tinder on the almost extinct fire. By the ensuing light, he dressed and then started wrapping up his few possessions in his tanned deer hides. He rolled everything together in two big bundles. He decided to leave his stone jug and the heavy cast iron pot and pan. He took the saw and corn knife along with his spears and bow and arrows. All of his tanned hides were rolled together along with the winter clothing he had made. He scooted his possessions through the opening and stood looking around inside the tree. It already looked vacant and lonely.

Smokey, who had been out sniffing around and marking his territory in dog fashion, came back inside. He was already moving more easily than he had the day before. His scars were still red and somewhat inflamed, but it had become apparent that he would survive. Even Smokey seemed to sense that they were leaving the tree for good. A few tears slid down David's cheek as he crawled out of the tree for the last time. He wondered what someone would think if they ever looked inside the tree and saw the remains of his habitation.

The sun was just peeking over the horizon when Sam and Charley bumped the big dugout canoe into the roots of the old sycamore. David handed down his bundles, then carefully picked up the big dog and handed him to Charley in the front of the canoe. Smokey didn't protest, but seemed uneasy in the wobbly craft. David carefully stepped into the center of the canoe and sat on one of his bundles of hides. The canoe also contained two big bundles of dried meat, barely leaving David enough room to sit.

Charley pushed the canoe back from the tree and Sam expertly paddled to the middle of the river with an economy of strokes. The other heavily-laden canoes were shoving off as well. Sam and Charley dug in with their paddles and shot ahead to the lead position. In seconds, the canoe entered the first riffle and the current took over and the speed picked up. Smokey stood up and barked, making the canoe wobble from side to side as they headed swiftly downstream.

The river was a series of holes of relatively slow current that ended with a riffle where the river would suddenly drop several feet. The boys would paddle through the slow holes, then simply navigate through the rapids using the paddle in the rear as a tiller. Occasionally, there would be a large rock or a log in the riffle that would require some swift maneuvering with the paddles to avoid getting hung up or tipping over. At these times, David would cling to the sides of the canoe and hold on until his knuckles were white. It was his first ride in a boat except for simply crossing a stream. The experience of racing along with the current was new and exciting. Smokey, although still weak and not fully recovered, seemed to thoroughly enjoy it as well.

Traveling along the river so quietly allowed them to get very close to a lot of wildlife that would normally be frightened away on land. Wood ducks would take wing at the last minute, rising up almost under the bow of the canoe. Great blue herons would sometimes stand in the water fishing and let the canoe pass by within a few feet. Other times, they would flap their ungainly wings and glide down stream to light, only to take off again as the boat approached. White limestone bluffs rose alternately on one side of the river or the other; some were hundreds of feet high with caves and holes visible high on their sides. Cedar trees clung to the sides of the bluff in places where it looked as if there was no soil to nourish their roots. Occasionally a deer would be drinking at the edge, and once a doe with two spotted fawns stood and curiously watched as the strange boats floated quietly by.

Cliff swallows darted across the water, sometimes skimming the top of the water to get a drink. Usually they were busy capturing small insects to feed their brood, waiting impatiently in mud nests stuck on the cliffs in sheltered caves and under overhangs. A large turkey gobbler took wing and flew across the river, passing directly across the canoe and only a few feet above. Vultures rode the wind currents around the steep bluffs, and nested high among the ledges in areas that could only be reached by flight. Small mammals were busy as well. Gray squirrels and red fox squirrels were abundant, and beaver, muskrat, raccoons, and even mink could be seen through the early morning mist that still clung to the valley.

The leaves on the trees were still bright green and new looking, not yet fully grown. Gravel bars along the river were blanketed with wildflowers: purple violets, Red Indian paintbrush. There were many pink and white flowers too, most of which David could not identify. The redbud trees were past their peak, but the dogwood, wild plum, and hawthorn were blooming profusely.

The river itself was clear and pristine. Fish were abundant and many times could be seen slowly swimming along in the crystal clear water. Turtles lay on logs where they had climbed out of the clear, cold water to sun themselves. Soft-shelled turtles with leathery-looking backs and pointed noses glided away from the boat. Some of the turtles they saw sunning themselves in the deep, quiet holes were huge with ridges down their back. These large snapping turtles seemed more wary than the smaller ones and would slip quietly from their perch as the canoes approached. Some of these snappers were bigger around than a washtub and their heads were bigger than two fists put together. They were equipped with sharp, wicked-looking beaks.

The group stopped to stretch their legs and drink from a spring of very cold water that gushed from a crack in a bluff. David could not believe how fast the morning had gone by; the sun was already directly overhead.

David asked Sam, "How far is it to your village?"

"Camp tonight, be there before dark tomorrow," he replied.

After a short rest and a meal of dried jerky, it was back in the canoes for the next leg of the journey. Once again, the boys took the lead. Their dugout canoe was not loaded as heavily as those paddled by the others. The more experienced men were carrying most of the meat. If one of the canoes should tip over, the dried meat would be ruined by the adsorption of the river water and would be useless to them. They had worked too hard to chance losing their hard-earned provisions.

The boys stayed far enough ahead that they only caught glimpses of the rest of the flotilla behind them on the long, straight stretches of the river. This added to their sense of adventure and made them feel as if they were alone. David, sitting in the middle of the canoe, had the luxury of taking in the view with no responsibility for paddling. Occasionally they would see snakes basking on the rocks or even coiled in the limbs of the willows that overhung the river. Sam and Charley carefully avoided passing underneath any of the low overhanging branches; they seemed to have a very healthy respect for the dark-colored, heavy-bodied snakes they occasionally passed.

"White mouth snake very bad temper. Sometimes he chase you if you disturb him sleeping. If snake bite you, most time you die. Get very sick, swell up, skin split, turn black. You die, two days maybe." Charley was not fond of these dangerous reptiles.

David had heard of the infamous cottonmouth snake, but had never seen one before. The White River, with which he was more familiar, was said to be inhabited by cottonmouth snakes. They seemed, however, to be pretty rare. It seemed they were anything but rare on the Buffalo Fork.

They reached an area where the river dropped rapidly in a short distance. It narrowed considerably and a small pool of water followed each riffle. In turn, that pool of water was followed by another riffle, and so on for several hundred yards. The swift flow of water kept Charley and Sam busy trying to control the heavy canoe. There were lots of rocks to dodge and sharp turns in the channel. They came out of one sharp turn and turned down what appeared to be the main channel. The river had split into three narrow branches that each found its own way through the gravel to the next hole of water. They chose the chute that flowed against the south bank, as it seemed to be deeper and carry the heaviest volume of water. That seemed to be the right choice, except the chute narrowed to a width of only four feet and was completely overhung by drooping trees and bushes. Suddenly Charley, who was in the bow, ducked as low in the boat as he could go and yelled, "Snake!"

David heard the sound of something heavy falling onto the bag between himself and Smokey. He was ducking to avoid the tree limbs as well and it took him a couple of seconds to realize that there was a very angry dusky-colored snake only an arm's length in front of him. The snake immediately coiled on top of the deerskin bag and opened his large mouth to expose a lethal-looking set of dripping fangs and the pure white interior of his mouth. David immediately bailed out of the boat into the water. His sudden move almost swamped the boat. Sam and Charley fought for balance as they tried to right the canoe. David had barely avoided the strike of the angry snake, which wasted no time in following David into the water. David saw the snake go into the water only a few feet from him, and fought the swift current to stay upstream from it. The snake was much more at home in the water than was David, and headed straight for him, moving swiftly on top of the water.

David strove for the rocky bank, half walking, half swimming, trying valiantly to stay ahead of the angry snake. He reached the bank first and scrambled out of the water, just ahead of the snake, barely avoiding the striking snake. As he scrambled onto dry land, he looked to see the snake still coming after him. He backed up a few feet and looked for a weapon with which to defend himself. There was nothing handy except some fist-sized rocks mixed in with the sand, gravel, and mussel shells that crunched under his feet. He grabbed a couple of rocks and started pummeling the snake with rock after rock as quickly as he could pick them up. One lucky blow with a fist-sized rock caught the snake in the middle of the back and broke its back. It continued to hiss in defiance and strike out with its venomous fangs until more rocks connected with its head and stopped the onslaught.

David hit the snake with a few more rocks just to be on the safe side, then stopped to catch his breath and try to control his shaking. He looked up to see the boys running toward him. They had managed to get the canoe safely to the next large pool of water about a hundred yards further down the river.

The boys came running up at about the same time the other canoes arrived at the top of the riffle. Everyone beached their canoes and ran toward David. David was bent over the snake, trying to catch his breath from the exertion.

"You bit?" shouted Sam.

Charley, being less optimistic, asked, "Where he hit you?"

"I'm all right," gasped David. "It was close, but I managed to stay out of his reach."

"Make sure. Sometime don't hurt now," said Hawk, as he looked closely at David's hands and arms, then checked around his legs and ankles.

Everyone now turned their attention to the big snake. The dark-colored snake was about three feet long, thick-bodied and blunt-tailed. There were indistinct markings on the back that formed a mottled, dusky, diamond-shaped pattern. The head was broad and spade shaped, but seemed small in proportion to the body. The inside of the mouth was snow white with large, curved fangs. Even in death, the large moccasin looked menacing. It was late in the afternoon, so everyone agreed that the large gravel bar would make a good campsite. The rest of the canoes were carefully floated down the chute to the large hole of water and beached on the sand and gravel bar for the night.

No shelter was constructed. Some brush was laid on top of the gravel to keep the bags of dried meat from directly touching the ground so they would not draw moisture. Driftwood was dragged up for a fire and everyone gathered around to talk about the snake and the other adventures of the day.

Lone Elk caught a few large catfish and they were roasted whole over the fire. His method of catching fish was a technique David had never seen before. Lone Elk stripped naked and waded into the river. David had presumed he intended to bathe. Instead he had waded into water that was about chest deep until he found one of the large submerged rocks that were plentiful in the river. Some of these rocks were huge boulders that had fallen from the cliffs over the eons and now offered shelter and hiding places for the large catfish that hunted their prey at night. Lone Elk would feel around the side of the rock with his bare feet until he located a hole underneath or on the side of the rock. He would then take a deep breath and submerge his entire body, sticking his hand back into the hole until he felt a fish. When the fish attacked his hand, he would stick his hand into the fish's mouth and slide his fingers out through the gill plates so he could grasp the slippery fish. He would then stand up and wade to shore with the wildly flapping fish and heave it up on the bank.

The last fish that he caught was so large that he had trouble regaining his feet and the battle lasted for several minutes with Lone Elk raising his head up for air then being pulled back under by the thrashing fish. When the fish finally succumbed, Lone Elk waded to shore, dragging a fish that weighed at least 30 pounds. His arm was rubbed raw by the rough jaws of the large fish, and blood mixed with water was dripping from his arm. In spite of the pain, he had a huge grin on his face; apparently pleased with himself for besting the catfish in its own element.

The catfish was a yellowish-brown in color with a very flat head and a long whisker at each corner of its mouth. The large mouth was more than big enough to place both fists in side-by-side.

David was impressed and excited, but after his experience with the snake, he had no desire to stick his hand underneath a rock. He had also seen several of the giant snapping turtles that sunned themselves along the river. This method of fishing held no appeal for him.

Everyone had their fill of fresh-roasted catfish as the sun faded from the sky in a spectacular display of orange and pink hues. There was a warm breeze blowing from the south, and only a few wispy clouds moved north with the breeze. A full belly and a crackling fire were making David very sleepy. The fire was more for enjoyment than need, but later, as the fog began to settle into the valley, it helped dispel the chill. Sleeping under the stars on a warm night was an enjoyable experience. The night sounds were beginning to fill the air around them. The lonely call of the whippoorwill was David's favorite night sound, but the frogs and crickets were the most noisome, seeming to compete with each other to see who could be the loudest.

The bellow of the big green bullfrog seemed to win most of the time, but the cacophony created by the numerous species of frogs wafted back and forth, sometimes quieting in one place and increasing in another, up and down the river. The tree frogs would appear to take the lead occasionally, with a chorus of spring peepers chiming in with their high-pitched calls. There was so much to listen to that sleep was hard to come by. The water was alive with sound as well. The musical chime of the water flowing over rocks was often interrupted by the splash of a fish jumping to capture a hapless bug, or some other unnamed critter attempting to make a meal out of another critter. Fireflies were numerous, a dancing cloud of blinking lights that swirled around in a dance that almost seemed rehearsed. The stars were exceptionally bright, as the moon had not yet risen in the eastern sky.

Old Crow was in a mood for talking, and storytelling around a campfire seemed completely appropriate. David drifted off to sleep listening to the old man telling an ancient tale of how his ancestors had come into being; a story that had passed by word of mouth, from generation to generation. His broken English was easy to understand, but his use of the correct verbs and adjectives made his version seem very foreign.

"Once before earth covered with all kinds of creatures," began the old man, "man and most creatures lived under the ground. All men lived forever, never sick. It dark place, no light; man groped around under ground, eating roots and worms. One day eating roots, first man crawled up inside giant tree and looked out on world through knothole. Him saw light, green trees, flowers. It beautiful place; every day after, he crawl into tree. Every day he look at world through knothole. He bring woman, show her beautiful things; they longed to live in beautiful place. Not grovel under ground, they were afraid. One day, great storm blow off top of tree. First man crawled up into tree, stuck head up out of stump, looked all about. Great vulture come, sit on edge of stump, told him he had choose. Stay under ground live forever. Come out into world, days of life be short, would grow old and die. Although short, days would be filled with beauty, would have many children, live in the light. First man went back and talked to wife, and other creatures that lived under ground. Wife agreed, better live in light for short while, than live forever in dark. The other creatures like fox and bear, and wolf and deer all decided live in light also. They all crawled up through tree stump, joined birds and fishes that already lived in air and water. Some creatures, like mole, decided to stay underground. Other creatures could not make up their mind and spend part of time underground, like bear and groundhog. Now man lives in light, much happier, even though his days are much shorter. This is how man and all animals came to live on earth."[17]

Everyone remained silent after the old man finished speaking. All but David had heard the story many times and quietly contemplated man's lot because of decisions made by their ancestors. David went to sleep and dreamed fitfully that his old sycamore tree was an entrance into the underworld.

Chapter Twelve

The next morning, David awoke to the sound of birds calling to each other as the light returned to the sky. Tom turkeys gobbled as they attempted to collect their harems at the start of the day. A mist of fog lay over the river like a fluffy blanket as everyone began to stir. The fire was built up to dispel the chill, and everyone quietly found something to eat while the sun dried up the fog. This morning, everyone went to the river and bathed, putting on their best clothes and tying back their hair with colorful bands of cloth. David did not have much choice in his wardrobe, but decided that his one remaining shirt, worn with his deerskin britches, would have to suffice. Sam brought him a blue strip of cloth to roll up and make into a headband to tie back his now long blond hair. Sam and Charley had put on their own best attire and nodded approvingly at David.

Everyone loaded into the canoes and started down the river as soon as the fog had lifted. Even Smokey, who was getting stronger every day, seemed to feel the excitement that the others transmitted.

The river now had widened and moved slower. The holes of water were longer with fewer riffles separating them. The water was crystal clear, revealing huge rocks lying just under the surface. Occasionally, the top of one of the huge rocks stuck a few inches above the water, creating a sunning platform for the myriad of turtles. Along the edge of the bluff that bordered the east bank of the river, huge boulders--some the size of houses--had broken from the bluff and tumbled to the river's edge. These huge boulders, interspersed with white-barked sycamore trees flanking the clear-flowing river, created a scene of beauty unequaled in nature. The canoes rounded a bend that curved more to the east, and the excitement level increased again. There was a long, straight stretch of river ahead that culminated in a shoal where there was a large gap in the bluff on the left. Another valley intersected the river from the east.

A race quickly developed between the heavy dugout canoes. Everyone dug in with their paddles and strained against the water to increase their speed. The current was slow and offered little assistance. The canoe paddled by Hawk and Bull That Roars was one of the more heavily laden, but they were also two of the strongest. They quickly drew alongside the boys in the lighter canoe and matched them stroke for paddle stroke. Even Smokey got excited. Standing directly behind Charley in the bow of the canoe, he started barking encouragement. David didn't have a paddle, but offered what little help he could contribute by using his hands as paddles.

Youth prevailed, and the smaller canoe pulled far enough ahead to suddenly veer into a small, quiet stream that entered from the left. There were a couple of excited squeals from small children, and a group of women and children came running to the bank as the canoes slid to a gravel-crunching halt against the bank. Hawk was the first ashore. Two small girls squealed with delight and grabbed onto his legs, one attaching herself to his left leg, the other to his right. Their beaming mother, a statuesque brown-skinned lady in a fringed doeskin dress waited patiently for her turn to greet him. All around David, greetings were being exchanged as happy families were reunited. He was feeling a little sad and left out, knowing he could not share that experience of homecoming with his own family. Everyone was talking so fast and excitedly in their native tongue that David had no idea what was being said, but their faces easily conveyed the universal language of happiness.

Suddenly, everyone stopped and looked directly at him, noticing him for the first time. Although dressed much like they were, his blond hair, blue eyes, and fair skin made him stand out, once noticed. David stood quietly, holding Smokey's lead rope and feeling very self-conscious. Everyone pressed in close for a better look and he found himself surrounded by inquisitive but not unfriendly faces.

Old Crow took the lead and announced, "Bring back Boy Who Lived in Tree and Slays Bear, and his brave dog. Both are great warriors and hunters. He travels to his uncle's house on Richland Creek. We take him in few days, trade with white men at Woollum." Everyone seemed satisfied with the explanation, but still curious. Everyone grabbed a load from the canoes; even the smallest toddlers helped to carry small bundles. David got his bundle from the canoe and someone instantly took it from him, a tall, slender girl about his age. She motioned for him to follow with Smokey and took off up the trail as if his bundle weighed nothing. David was embarrassed that a girl was carrying his heavy load, but there was nothing to do but follow.

The trail led up the bank to a large, cultivated field. Already young corn was sprouting, and bean and squash vines were starting to put out their tender shoots. The field was well tended, and patches of various vegetables were laid out in straight rows covering the field. On the upper side of the field, along the edge of the timber, stood a row of well-built cabins. There were a half dozen of them, all built essentially the same. They were double cabins with a breezeway or dog run between. They were made of hewn and notched logs, much like those built by white settlers. There was a common area between the two middle cabins that surrounded a huge pecan tree. There were logs to sit on, and a fire pit surrounded by a ring of flat stones. It was obviously a communal meeting place. Everyone gathered there in the shade of the huge tree.

A wooden bucket of ice cold spring water was brought by one of the women, and a gourd dipper was passed around for everyone to drink from. The dried meat was stacked up on a platform of flat rocks and everyone gathered around; an impromptu feast seemed to materialize. One of the women brought a huge wooden platter filled with freshly-picked wild strawberries. Stew pots were brought from houses and small fires kindled to heat the various stews and other dishes. In a matter of minutes, a huge meal was being served.

The meal consisted of corn, beans, and squash. A platter of stewed greens included a mixture of vegetables that David could not identify, but contained polkweed and dandelion, as well as shoots from cattail and various other greens. It was seasoned with a little bear fat and was delicious. There was fresh fish and turtle soup as well as stewed meat of various kinds. One pot contained thick white soup, small pieces of freshwater clams, and fish along with corn. Corn cakes were served covered in honey. The girl who carried his pack brought him a huge wooden platter filled with all of these delights. David ate so much, he thought he was going to be sick.

After everyone had eaten their fill, the storytelling began. Old Crow started the process, recounting their trip up the river, the building of their hunting camp, and their successful hunt. Most of this was stated in his broken English, which everyone seemed to understand. Occasionally, he had to fill in with his native tongue to get a point across, but enough was spoken in English that David could follow along. When he got to their discovery of David's presence, everyone listened more intently. When he recounted the tale of the bear hunt, there were exclamations of disbelief and astonishment. Crow had David stand beside him, and he took the necklace of bear claws from around his neck and passed them around for everyone to see. The size of the claws made an impression, and both David and Smokey were looked on with new respect and awe.

When he recounted their trip back home, the story of the snake falling into the boat was greeted with laughter. David's quick exit from the boat was described in great detail, and embellished to sound as if he had flown across the water so quickly that he hardly got wet. The story was told to paint a mental picture of David fleeing from the little snake in panic after standing up to the huge bear. David was a little embarrassed, but realized it was all in good fun. The storytelling continued well into the night with everyone taking a turn at describing his experiences and impressions. Finally everyone looked at David, and he realized it was his turn to tell his story and explain his reason for living alone in the tree.

David stood and formally introduced himself. "My name is David, David Christian. I used to live in Missouri, near a small village called Springfield. My mother and baby sister died a few years ago, leaving just me and my father. I helped my father farm and hunt and trap. Last fall, he was felling a tree to clear another field, when it suddenly split and fell toward us. My father was able to push me out of the way, but a large limb came down on him and broke his back."

The entire group was solemnly watching him in sympathy as a few tears rolled down his cheek. "Before he died, my father told me to go live with his younger brother Darrell after I sold the farm. The next day, some men came from town and helped me bury my father next to my mother and sister. One of the men, the constable, said our farm would be great for his sister and brother-in-law, who were looking for a place. I told him I would consider selling it to them and go live with my Uncle Darrell. He laughed and said he would send them out to see the place. The next day, they showed up with a wagon filled with kids and very few possessions, and told me they were moving in to take care of me. They immediately moved into the cabin and took over the place. The woman told me they had an order from the Justice of the Peace to take possession of the place as my guardian. I was given a blanket and told to make a bed in the barn. She said their children were smaller and sickly, and needed to be in the house and there just wasn't enough room for me inside.

"That night I left with what little I could take with me, hoping that I could make it to Uncle Darrell's before the weather got bad. I ran out of food, and a big snowstorm caught up with me just as I reached the Buffalo River and I was lucky that Smokey caught a big 'coon that lived in the hollow sycamore tree or I might have starved or frozen to death. I lived in the tree the rest of the winter and was getting ready for the next leg of my journey when I was captured by your hunting party."

Everyone laughed about his capture and the tension was broken. David felt much better, having shared his experiences with his newfound friends. The girl who had carried his packs and served his meal stepped forward and handed David a blanket and said, "David can stay in barn for as long as he likes." Everyone laughed at the joke and David, quite embarrassed, took the blanket and stood quietly as everyone patted him on the back and introduced themselves. The only one he remembered for sure was the girl's name, Mary. She was Charlie's sister.

It was late and the celebration broke up with David feeling like he had acquired a complete new family. His friends, Sam and Charley, led him toward one of the cabins and joked that they would show him to the barn. But instead they led him to the breezeway of one of the houses. His pack lay against the wall on one side and Charley told him that they liked to sleep out here when the weather was nice. Smokey seemed content to be here, and had grown accustomed to the Indians.

Already, David had trouble thinking of them as Indians. They lived much the same as his own people. The women mostly wore colorful cotton dresses and everyone was clean and polite. The family interactions were the same as any other family he had been around. The speech was different, but he was getting used to it and hardly noticed the lack of some adjectives that he took for granted. Everyone, even the youngest children, seemed to have a fairly good grasp of English. David spread out his deerskin sleeping mat on the packed earth floor and using his pack for a pillow, stretched out beside Sam and Charley. The whippoorwills and frogs quickly sang him to sleep.

David awoke to the crowing of a rooster and got up to find a place of privacy to answer to his bodily needs. The fog was heavy over the little valley and quiet had settled over the earth, as if the night creatures had given up on the night, but the creatures of daylight had yet to awaken. It was a beautiful, serene morning; dew was heavy on the grass and just enough light was filtering over the mountains to the east to reveal the blanket of white fog that lay over the river as it wound its way to the southeast. The waning moon was still hanging low in the western sky, adding to the light, and a few of the brightest stars were still visible.

As David walked back to the cabin, he noticed that a few others were starting to move about as well. A woman left one house carrying a water bucket toward the spring; another was rekindling a fire. From somewhere came the sound of wood chopping as someone prepared wood for the morning cooking fire. It was the first time David had heard the sounds of civilization in a long time. It felt good to be among people again.

Sam and Charley were awake and stretching as David made his way back to the breezeway. Even Smokey was up, nosing around the yard lifting his leg as he marked the trees and bushes others of his kind had marked before him. A handful of dogs of various colors and shapes warily circled him while he disdainfully ignored them.

David asked what he could do to help, and Mary walked out of the house and handed him a wooden bucket. Without saying a word, she pointed toward the trail to the spring, turned, and re-entered the house. Sam and Charley laughed at David and started to tease him, saying that Mary already had him as well trained as a husband. David turned red and headed for the spring.

Breakfast was not an elaborate meal. It consisted of a black and bitter brew somewhat resembling coffee, and hot corn cakes covered with honey. David enjoyed the sweet honey and wasted no time in downing his cakes. Soon the women and girls had their hoes in hand and were off to the fields before the sun had dried up the fog. One old woman sat down cross-legged by a large flat stone with a rounded indentation in the surface. She shelled some corn from the cob and began to pound and grind the corn into a fine meal. The hard, round rock that she used as a grindstone was smooth and polished from many hours of work. Some of the men went off to cut wood, leading a crudely harnessed old horse to drag the logs back to the village. There seemed to be very few farm animals about. Only two horses were in evidence. There were no pigs, sheep, or goats; only chickens, and not a lot of them.

David asked Sam and Charley why there were no farm animals. Sam replied, "Plenty of animals in forest, take care of selves. Eat acorns and plants and get fat from land. We want meat, we go to forest, no need for keep animals, have to feed them like white men do. Crow say we should have farm animals and learn to care for them, that someday soon, animals all be gone from forest, have to be prepared. He say it happened same way where we live before."

"Where did you live before?" asked David.

"When we were small, we lived far away in place called Ten-a-see. Had big village, grew much corn, had many horses, pigs, and chickens. One day, soldiers came, said we had to move to Indian Territory. Some of our tribe wanted to fight soldiers, but there were too many. We were forced to load a few things into one wagon and leave everything else behind. White men moved into our houses as we leave. We traveled many days through cold winter; many of our people die from cold or coughing sickness. Others die crossing big rivers. Soldiers beat us and stole things from us until nothing left. One night, during big storm, some of us slip away, taking only what we could carry. We traveled south for many days until we found this valley. Have been here ever since. No one has bothered us. Figure someday, soldiers come again, make us leave. Maybe then we be many, strong enough to fight. Old Crow says must become like white men. Speak English, dress like white people, marry white people. Only way to survive is become white. The day of the red man is gone forever. Hope he is wrong."

David felt empathy for their plight, having been put out of his own house.

"We will find a bee tree today," said Charley. "We are almost out of honey and need to refill our barrels."

Sam went into the cabin, returning with a small piece of honeycomb glistening with raw honey dripping from its waxy cells. He placed it on a piece of tree bark and licked the sticky honey from his fingers. He led the way out into the field, walking between the rows of beans and squash until he found a small patch of wild blackberry briars at the edge of the field closest to the river. They were in full bloom and hundreds of honeybees were buzzing about, crawling over the white blooms, collecting pollen and nectar to carry back to their hive. Sam placed the piece of bark containing the honey on a bare spot of ground a few feet from the thorny vines. The three boys then squatted down and started to watch.

Honeybees are not native to North America, but had been brought from Europe by early settlers. Finding few natural enemies and an abundance of food, they had quickly spread over most of the continent, particularly the southern half of what would become the continental United States. For the most part, they built their hives in the cavities of hollow trees that were abundant in the old growth deciduous forests that covered most of the continent. The Indians sometimes referred to them as Whiteman's flies, and quickly developed a taste for the honey.

It did not take long for the bees to find the bit of honey. First one, then many were crawling over the honeycomb and gorging on the honey. They were soon so full, they could hardly fly and would laboriously take to wing, making a beeline directly toward their hive. Being fully gorged, they had no need to continue flying from flower to flower, but instead would take the most direct path back to their hive. All of the bees did not go in the same direction, since they were from different hives. By watching carefully, the boys were able to determine that the majority of the bees headed off from the piece of bark in the same direction. They would lift off clumsily, make a couple of small circles to orient themselves, and head out on exactly the same flight path. By positioning themselves directly behind the bees, they were able to follow their flight across the field in the early morning light, and sight along their flight path, much like sighting a gun.

It was easy to determine that the bees were heading toward the side of the first tall ridge to the east of the field and about two-thirds of the way to the top. Sam stayed behind to sight along the beeline, and sent Charley and David across the field to the edge of the woods. They were then able to calculate which tree the bee passed over when exiting the field. David then stood at the edge of the field and Charley used his position to align himself with Sam as he ascended the hill. The growth was so thick that after entering the forest, it was hard to determine which tree might contain the hive.

After Charley had determined the general area and narrowed the search to a handful of trees, all three boys started carefully watching the openings in the canopy, looking for bees crossing the openings. Suddenly, Charley pointed and whistled to draw attention to the way he was looking. The boys gathered around and started to observe a bee passing through the opening every few seconds and flying directly toward the same tree. It was a big white oak scarred by an ancient fire. The tree had lost a few limbs to wind and lightning strikes. Several knotholes showed evidence that the tree was hollow.

The boys looked around the base of the tree and discovered several dead bees lying on the ground in one general area. When bees died in the hive, they would immediately be carried to the opening and pushed out of the hive by worker bees in charge of keeping the hive clean. They backed up to get a better angle for viewing the top of the tree, and soon picked out the knothole that the bees were entering. It was a very busy hive. Hundreds of bees were continually entering and exiting the tree. The bark around the opening was worn smooth and shiny from the constant use.

"This should be good honey tree. I start chopping. You go bring buckets, old rag for smoking. I have tree ready to fall by time you return," stated Sam.

It was less than half a mile back to the village, and by the time they returned, Sam was sitting on the ground, building a small fire a few feet from the tree. The tree had been hollow all the way to the base, and Sam had chopped through the outer shell of the old tree, revealing the cavity inside. Only about one-third of the trunk remained to support the tree on the uphill side; a slight breeze could easily make it fall. Fortunately there was no wind. David, understandably, was a little leery around large trees that were getting ready to fall, and stayed well back from the tree on the uphill side.

When Sam had the fire going well, he raked up a pile of dead leaves from the ground and started stuffing them into the cavity of the tree. He then lit the leaves with a burning branch. Slowly, the old tree started acting as a natural chimney as the hot smoky air rose inside the cavity, and smoke started pouring through the knotholes further up the tree. The boys pulled on long-sleeved buckskin shirts and tied bands around their wrists and pant legs. They improvised hoods by tying other shirts over their heads, exposing as little of their bodies as possible in order to prevent stings by angry bees.

Suddenly, addled bees started pouring from the hive, emerging from several holes. Most of the bees were too sick to fly, and crawled around on the trunk; others fell to the ground, kicking feebly with their feet in the air. Others buzzed around the opening, greatly disturbed. Sam wrapped a piece of the old cloth rag around a stick and laid the end in the edge of the fire to smolder. He then resumed chopping at the base of the now charred tree trunk. The tree quickly started to groan as the remaining fibers broke from trying to support its weight.

With a final snap and groan, the top of the old tree, losing its battle with gravity, slowly pitched down the hill, gaining momentum as it fell. With a crash, it landed on its side amid a shower of leaves that its branches had knocked from adjoining trees in its fall. The hollow trunk split open on impact, exposing several feet of honeycomb laden with golden liquid honey. Sam grabbed the smoldering torch from the fire and started waving it around the honeycomb to discourage any remaining bees. Not many bees put up a fight, but the boys all got a few stings robbing the honey. They filled six wooden buckets and still did not get all of the honey. Much leaked onto the ground and was lost. The boys filled their buckets then cut a piece of comb each and sat around their small fire, using the smoke to discourage any remaining hostile bees while they enjoyed the fruits of the bees' labor, being well compensated for the few stings they had received.

Chapter Thirteen

The next few days flew by. David enjoyed the time spent with his new friends. The days were spent fishing, swimming, and exploring the various creeks and valleys. The boys wrestled and ran races and competed with their bows. Hawk taught David how to make flint points for his arrows by pressing off flakes with the sharp point of a deer antler. Hawk could knock off a large flake from a flint core and have it shaped into a perfect point in just a few minutes. He would lay the flake on his knee on top of a stiff piece of leather and press off small flakes, alternating sides until the point was sharp and shaped to his liking. It took David a full day to make his first one that was useable. It was a little crude and thicker than the ones Hawk made, but he was extremely pleased with himself. He made several more over the next few days and gradually got better and faster, but knew he could never learn to do it as artistically as Hawk.

Smokey grew better quickly and was soon ready to resume hunting; he started to follow the boys everywhere they went. David was reluctant to leave, but was anxious to see his uncle, and Smokey was ready for the trip as well. David had been assured it was only one day of travel to his uncle's farm, and that knowledge spurred his anxiety to finish his journey. He told Sam and Charley that he needed to depart soon.

The next day, Lone Elk told him that they would make the journey the following day. That night, there was a big feast and party in David's honor, followed by much storytelling and lengthy good-byes. Everyone in the village had a few words to say to him, and everyone gave him a small gift, except Mary. She did not attend the festivities and stayed out of sight the entire evening.

Hawk gave him a beautiful flint knife hafted with antler in a beaded buffalo hide case. Most of the gifts were small packets of specially made treats. Sam and Charley gave him a small bucket made of tree bark and filled with some of the fresh honey.

David had little to give, but had made some wooden whistles for the children that his father had taught him to make from the hollow stems of the elderberry bush. He gave his bone fish spear to Charley and his spear made from the old knife to Sam. He presented his corn knife solemnly to Old Crow and gave his best mink skin to Hawk. He had a small gift that he had made, or a skin he had tanned for each member of the tribe. He knew that he would not need these things by the end of the following day.

For Mary, he had made a necklace of the very best flint arrow point he had made. It was an unusual color, gray with pink stripes marbled through it. He had flanked it with two small delicate pink shells that he had found on the river bank. He was especially proud of this gift, but Mary seemed to be avoiding him completely. As the night grew later, he kept watching for Mary and could think of little else. He finally went to sleep on the breezeway, aware that there was a dim light shining inside Mary's cabin all night.

The next morning, he was the first to awaken, having not slept very well. He quietly arose and started packing up his few remaining personal effects. He had very little left to pack--only his bow and quiver of arrows, his axe, and a small pack containing a few items of clothing, along with the small canvas bag that held his knives and fire starting material. It didn't take long to assemble his possessions. He didn't even plan on taking his sleeping mat and cover.

By the time he was finished, Sam and Charley were getting up and making ready to travel as well. Lone Elk and Bull That Roars had assembled their packs of trade goods and were standing under the big pecan tree waiting to leave. David looked around for Mary one more time and reached in his canvas pack, removed the necklace wrapped in a soft piece of doeskin, and tied with a bow. He handed it to Charley and said, "Give this to Mary for me. I didn't see her all day yesterday."

Charley nodded his head in the direction behind David and said, "Give it to her yourself, she is standing behind you."

David turned and beautiful Mary was standing just outside the door holding something in her hands. She looked very tired, but was dressed in her best white doeskin dress with fringes and beadwork. She was tall and slender with tragic doe eyes looking at David.

"I'm sorry that I not speak to you last night," she said. "But I had to work very hard to finish your gift in time and I was afraid it would not be finished if I stopped for even a short time." She held up the most beautiful shirt David had ever seen. It was made of doeskin and tanned almost white. It was fringed along the bottom and the sleeves, with a scallop of fringe on the back. The front of the shirt was covered with a beautiful starburst design of yellow with red and blue rays emanating outward. The shirt was an elegant piece of artistry and workmanship. David was at such a loss for words that he stood there in mouth agaped awe. She handed him the shirt and stood there with her eyes downcast biting her lower lip. David handed her his small package and waited as she untied and unwrapped the necklace. Her tired eyes sparkled as she admired it and then placed it over her head.

"I will not take off until I see you again," she said softly and turned to walk back into the cabin.

David stood there not knowing what to say until a laughing Sam and Charley grabbed him by the arms and propelled him into the yard. He carefully folded the shirt and placed it inside his pack. It was far too nice to wear on a journey. Only the five of them were going to the trading post. Lone Elk and Bull That Roars wanted mainly powder and shot for their ancient rifles, and Sam and Charley, who carried a few skins to trade, were mostly along for the adventure.

They started toward the river, David expecting them to go to where the canoes were beached, but instead they crossed the river at the shallow ford just above the swift riffle and started down a trail that paralleled the river.

As if reading his mind, Charley told him, "River too swift here to bring canoe back up. Many shoals and much swift water first half day. When we reach big hole of water find another canoe, paddle rest of way." When the sun reached nearly the midpoint in the sky, they emerged on a gravel bar after crossing the river several times during the morning. The river appeared wider and flowed smoothly into the distance. A small creek entered on the left bank. It was lined with a thick stand of cane and was only about knee deep. They waded up the creek a short distance, and around a bend was what appeared to be a log laying half in and half out of the water. They waded up to the log and, grasping the sides, they turned it over to reveal a large dugout canoe that was over 20 feet long. Lone Elk waded into the cane a short distance, and returned with four paddles. Everyone busily started bailing the residual water from the canoe and wiping out the mud with leaves. Some mats were quickly woven from cane shoots and placed in the bottom of the canoe to keep the packs from absorbing moisture from the bottom of the still soggy canoe. The canoe was floated down to the river, and one by one they crawled in, resting on their knees in the bottom of the canoe--Lone Elk in the front, followed by Charley, then David and Smokey. Sam was next with Bull That Roars sitting in the stern. This canoe was larger than any they had used before. Four people paddling in unison fairly made the canoe fly through the water.

Once again, David was not given a paddle, and had only to sit still and enjoy the sights. The scenery at first was little different than the upper river, but soon that began to change. The bluffs, although not as tall, were spectacular. They rounded a bend and saw a huge, white bluff on their right that was sheer and smooth. At the base, a huge cave opened, large enough to paddle the canoe through the opening. A narrow crack pierced the bluff a little farther down. Light shining through showed the bluff to be a narrow ridge of rock that separated two large valleys.

"Richland Creek just on other side of bluff," said Lone Elk. "Almost come together here but can't get through rock. Not far now, we go to trading post first, see if uncle there. If not there, we go up Richland Creek to cabin, not far there."

David couldn't believe that his journey was near its end. Smokey sat still just in front of David, wagging his tail as if he knew as well.

They rounded a bend and saw smoke rising from a chimney. Civilization was in sight. There was a creek flowing into the river from both the left and right. The small creek on the left had several buildings situated on its bank. The creek had been dammed up and a wooden water wheel turned slowly in the flume of water shooting over the dam. A two-story log building stood next to the wheel. Another single-story log structure stood nearby. Several people were around the buildings as the canoe ground to a halt just above the shoal a couple of hundred yards from the buildings. It was too far to tell who any of the people might be.

Everyone in David's group grabbed their loads and waded across the creek toward the buildings. They had not yet been detected by those around the buildings. As they got closer and climbed the bank, someone finally noticed their appearance and called out, "Here come some Injuns, boys, watch your hair." Everyone stopped what they were doing and turned to watch. Some looked apprehensive and a couple of women cowered behind their husbands.

"We're here to trade with Robinson," said Lone Elk in his best English.

"He talks better than most Injuns," said the wag who had announced their presence.

A tall, white-haired man came to the door, wiping his hands on a stained apron. "Welcome, Lone Elk," he said. "It has been a long time since you were here. How is Old Crow doing? I see he is not with you."

"He sends his greetings, and a couple of fine deerskins to trade for tobacco," replied Lone Elk.

Everyone filed into the trading post behind Robinson, except David, who remained on the porch to look things over. He was more interested in the people than the goods inside the store.

There was a two-wheeled ox cart yoked to a team of spotted oxen standing in front. The oxen were placidly chewing their cud and swishing their tails at flies. The cart contained several sacks of freshly-milled corn meal. A baby and a little girl of about four sat in the bottom of the cart on a pallet of patchwork quilts and sacking. A man with a long beard and a washed-out-looking woman in a faded gingham dress and bonnet stood beside the cart, looking at David.

Three men stood under the shade of a large cottonwood tree. An anvil sat on a stump next to the tree, and a small fire was burning nearby. One of the men was obviously a blacksmith. He wore a leather apron and held a large hammer in one hand and a pair of tongs in the other. A smoking piece of metal was grasped in the jaws of the tongs. Everyone had stopped to stare at the Indians. One of the three was the loudmouthed wag who had announced the presence of the Indians.

"I wonder where the light-haired half-breed come from," he said to no one in particular.

David, having lived alone for months and for the last few weeks with people who treated him as a grown equal, forgot his size and age.

"I'm no half-breed," he answered. "Even if I were, I have better manners and upbringing than you seem to have."

The man turned red with rage and started toward David. "I'm gonna jerk a knot in your tail and teach you some manners, you little pup."

David took one step back and dropped everything but his axe. Suddenly, Smokey darted between the two with his teeth bared, a low, menacing growl erupting from his throat. The man stopped and started to curse. "Somebody throw me a club, I'm gonna kill me a dog and maybe a smart-mouthed boy."

Another man stepped out of the store. He was tall and slender with wavy, light brown hair. He wore buckskin breeches and a cotton shirt, and carried a long rifle. "What's happening, Earn?" he asked. "It looks like your big mouth has got you treed by a mean-looking dog. From the looks of things, he might have you for supper if he can stand the taste and get past the smell."

"Stay out of this, Christian. That boy deserves a whippin' and ain't no dog gonna tree me and live."

"Uncle Darrell, if he lays a hand on Smokey, I'll kill him myself."

Everyone froze. The tall man shifted his gaze to David and his mouth fell open. "My God, David, is that you?" he exclaimed in amazement. "I thought you were dead. I just got back from Springfield looking for you. No one claimed to have seen you since they buried your dad. The people living in the cabin claimed they had found the place abandoned and moved in. Said they knew nothing about a boy or who might have lived there before."

"Earn, back up from that dog real careful and get out of my sight. That's my nephew and his dog you're picking on, and I don't think you want to tangle with me."

The white-faced Earn carefully backed away and rounded the building out of sight. Seconds later, a horse was heard galloping away as fast as it could go.

Everyone had come out of the store and watched as David and his uncle Darrell hugged each other. Smokey got in on the act, wagging his tail and barking excitedly.

"Well, introduce me to your friends and tell me where you've been," said Darrell, as arm-in-arm they walked to the porch.

David's journey was over at last.

The End

(Endnotes)

[1] In the early 1800s, the last outpost of civilization--upstream or west--on the White River was a trading post owned by a family named Schell. They traded with early settlers and Indians indigenous to the area. The spelling has been changed, but the city that occupies this location is now known as Shell Knob, Missouri.

[2] According to the Newton County Arkansas Historical Society, the area was occupied by: Cherokee, Choctaw, Fox, Kickapoo, Sauk, and Osage tribes. The treaties of 1808 and 1818 split the Cherokee Nation. The area that became Newton County became part of the Western Cherokee, who wanted to preserve their heritage by avoiding contact with the whites. The Choctaw were the last legal landowners of the area before white settlement. By 1838, all of the remaining Native Americans had been assimilated into the white settlements. By 1840, when Newton County was formed from part of Marion County, the Indians had become landowners and accepted citizens by most folks. The first postmaster and county clerk in Newton County was John M. Ross. He served from 1842 to 1846. Mr. Ross was a Choctaw Indian.

[3] Persimmons are about the last fruit to ripen in the fall. They are inedible until after the first frost. Biting into an unripe persimmon leaves a horrible caustic taste in your mouth that will make your mouth pucker, and takes several minutes and much spitting to gain relief.

[4] Chinquapins no longer exist. A subspecies of the American chestnut, it was killed by the same blight that killed off the chestnut.

[5] Shawnee Town later became known as Yellville, Arkansas. Wild Bill Hickok later killed one of the Tutts in a gun battle over a card game there.

[6] According to the journals of Henry Rowe Schoolcraft, who spent the winter of 1818 and 1819 with settlers on the White River, game was exceedingly plentiful in the area. Deer, elk, bison, wild turkey, and black bear were easily available, and their skins were pretty much the currency of the time.

[7] Passenger pigeons were once the most numerous birds on the planet. Historians estimate that their numbers ranged from four to five billion birds. Individual flocks were sometimes one mile wide by three hundred miles long. They were as abundant and as seemingly inexhaustible as the huge herds of buffalo that existed on the plains. Market hunters killed them by the wagonload by knocking them out of the trees with sticks. The last known passenger pigeon died in the Cincinnati Zoo on September 1, 1914.

[8] The largest tree in the state of Missouri, until the spring of 2001, was a giant American sycamore that measured 291 inches in circumference. It stood on a farm near Jackson, Missouri. The tree was hollow and was used as a shelter for hogs. The tree had a diameter of over seven and one half feet and stood 112 feet tall with a crown that spread 200 feet across. Sadly, it was blown down by a tornado in the spring of 2001. (Source: Missouri Department of Conservation Web page and the owners, Mr. and Mrs. Norman Weiss.)

[9] A twitching stick was a common way to pull a small animal from its burrow. It is not uncommon for rabbits to crawl up inside a small hollow tree to escape from predators.

[10] Wringing a chicken's neck was a customary way of dispatching table fare.

¹¹ Richland Creek and Woollum still exist today. Woollum exists in name only as a popular access point to the Buffalo National River. It is a popular one-day float above the U.S. Highway 65 Bridge at St. Joe. Richland Creek is a scenic and pristine part of the Buffalo National River System.

¹² Mountain lions, also known as panthers, were once plentiful in the Ozarks. Thought to be extinct for about 100 years, there have recently been several documented reports of their existence in the Ozarks. Two apparently wild specimens have been killed by cars on Missouri highways during 2003. The Missouri Department of Conservation has documented another lion in the southern portion of the state near Fort Leonard Wood.

¹³ The wild cane referred to is actually a species of bamboo that was common throughout the Ohio and Mississippi valleys. The tender shoots were excellent forage for many game animals. In the spring, it was a favorite source of food for bears and people. The tender young shoots could be eaten raw or boiled and eaten as a vegetable. They were a great source of protein, minerals, and vitamins. They are still used as cane poles for fishing.

¹⁴ Gigging fish is still a popular sport in the Ozarks. The crystal clear streams make it easy to see fish plainly on the bottom in water as much as ten feet deep. Both Missouri and Arkansas have a gigging season in the fall and winter months. It is done mostly at night with the gigger standing on the front of a specially rigged johnboat with bright lights illuminating the water. Only rough fish may be taken in this manner, primarily carp and suckers.

¹⁵ Eastern red wolves were probably the most common native wolf to the Ozarks. They are somewhat larger than the average coyote, but

somewhat smaller than the gray or timber wolf. Red wolves have become very rare in the wild. Captive red wolves raised near St. Louis, Missouri at the Wolf Sanctuary have recently been reintroduced into the wild in the southeastern United States.

[16] Native Americans of the Cherokee and Choctaw tribes were taking names in the white tradition by the early nineteenth century, as exemplified by the names of some of the tribal leaders of this period like John Ross and Stand Watie.

[17] Every Native American tribe had its own creation story--some tribes even more than one--that explained their existence. This particular story is purely fiction, but many tribes believed they originated from under the ground.

About the Author

 Mitch Martin is a descendant of some of the earliest pioneers of the North Arkansas Ozarks region. He grew up on a small farm in Searcy County only a few miles from the scenic Buffalo National River. Hunting and fishing were not only a recreation but also a necessary part of everyday life. Mitch spent his early years hunting squirrels and rabbits with his .22 rifle and his dog Smokey. He learned to love the Buffalo River while fishing and hunting with his Uncle Charley Crow, a Choctaw Indian who made his living by farming with a team of mules, along with the sale of raccoon skins and wild ginseng root.

Mitch's unique experiences have allowed him to write a story that blends fiction with the everyday experiences of survival that faced early settlers in the region. Many of these skills have survived longer in the Ozarks than any other region of the country. Mitch is a member of a rapidly disappearing pioneer heritage group that can pass along firsthand knowledge of survival skills used by our ancestors.

Mitch is a graduate of Southwest Missouri State University in Springfield, Missouri where he received a degree in Wildlife Conservation and a ROTC commission as a Second Lieutenant in the U.S. Army Corps of Engineers. For the past twenty years he has worked in the financial services industry. He is the co-founder of a successful financial services firm in Washington, Missouri where he currently resides with his wife Candi. He is the father of two grown children, Jennifer and Jon. He loves hunting, fishing, camping and canoeing, especially on the Buffalo River.

Printed in the United States
22990LVS00001B/327